The Man Who Once Played Catch with NELLIE FOX

Published in 1998 by
Academy Chicago Publishers
363 West Erie Street
Chicago, Illinois 60654

First paperback edition 2009

Manufactured in the U.S.A.

Library of Congress Cataloging-in-Publication Data
on file with the publisher

ISBN 978-0-89733-597-3

The Man Who Once Played Catch with Nellie Fox

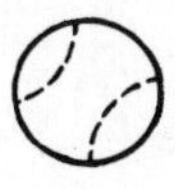

A Novel By John Manderino

Academy Chicago Publishers

To my mother and,
in loving memory, my father

Part One

Hank

1.

"Help! Help! The sky is falling!—"

Tommy, at his usual stool. He'd heard about the pop-up I dropped. Well, not really *dropped*.

"—The sky is falling! It hit me on the head!"

I sat at the other end of the bar and Larry brought me over an Old Style—Larry as in Jerry and Larry's Sports Palace, a big dim cool sticky room with a beat-up pool table and some pictures of Chicago athletes on the walls. It was Saturday, early yet, just Tommy there, Larry reading one of those newspapers about Bigfoot and Elvis Presley's ghost and babies born with a tail.

Tommy kept grinning at me, nodding his big bald head.

I told him to watch his game show and leave me the fuck alone.

Vanna White was turning over a bunch of O's. Tommy thinks she's some kind of goddess. I can't see it, myself. She's got a nice walk though, back and forth, swinging those arms.

"There's no fool like an old fool!" he shouted.

I figured he meant me, but he was telling the contestant the answer.

She ignored him and took another spin of the wheel and landed on Bankrupt.

"Stupid cow." He told Larry to put the Cub game back on.

I'll say this much for Tommy. Ever since we were kids he's always been a loyal Cubs fan. I don't know why. This is a *south* suburb, part of White Sox territory. I remember he once gave this other kid a pair of his sister's panties for an Ernie Banks card. They were red.

Sandberg took a called third strike.

"Swing the fucking bat," Tommy told him. Then he turned to me and smiled. "So, how's the old coconut?"

He enjoys himself. His life is even stupider than mine, but he enjoys it.

I asked him who he talked to. I knew he wasn't at the game, because if he's there you hear him. I do, anyway. He's always on my ass.

"Ossifer Phil."

This busybody cop, Phil Spaulding—my girlfriend Karen's cousin. Officer Phil, gossip squad.

"He said you could hear this *konk* when it landed," Tommy said, then started laughing his wheezy laugh, which turned into a coughing fit, till he gurgled something up, which he spit in a napkin. He smokes a lot.

In case you're interested, here's the way it happened. Eighth inning, guy hits a pop-up out to me at second base, a mile high against this big blank milky gray sky, and I start to get dizzy and jelly-legged, *two* balls coming down, and I go after the wrong one, the real ball bouncing off my head—with a *konk*—and landing behind me. Hurt like hell but I just went and picked it up and tossed it back to the pitcher and did some groundskeeping with my spikes—nobody laughing on either team, it was that pathetic. And when the inning was over I left the game. Just walked to my car and drove home.

Larry said, "Listen to this," and read to us from his newspaper, about a man in Milwaukee who ate his own cat.

Tommy defended the guy, meat being meat: "A cow, a cat, what the fuck's the difference?"

I thought about dropping by Karen's. Or staying here and getting shitfaced.

Tommy and Larry kept going at it about the guy and his cat.

I got up and left.

Tommy yelled, "Watch out for them falling baseballs!"

Karen answered the door all sweaty and redfaced in her spandex exercise suit, a Jane Fonda workout video carrying on behind her. Karen and Jane were wearing the same outfit, but what a difference. I'm saying Karen's gotten fat. Just in the last year or so she's gotten awful hefty.

First thing she says to me, "How's your head?"

"What the hell, was it on the news?"

She turned the video off. "Phil was over."

See what I mean about that guy?

"He said you left the game. Were you feeling dizzy? Or nauseous at all?" Karen's a part-time nurse's aid.

I sat on the couch and hung my head. "I left," I said, "because I'm forty years old and no damn good anymore. Washed up . . . over the hill . . ." I was waiting for her to come over and comfort me a little. "Obsolete . . . worthless . . ."

"Listen, Jim's on his way over, bringing Brian back, okay?"

Jim's her ex, Brian's their kid.

"Right," I said, and got up and trudged to the door.

"You can *stay*. I just thought you'd want to know."

I told her I'd see her later.

"Don't I even get a hug?" she said.

I went over and put my arms around her.

"What's the matter, Hank?"

"I don't know."

"Because you missed that ball?"

"I guess."

She held me tighter. "You're not over the hill, honey. You're a very good baseball player. Everyone makes an error once in a while. *You* know that. Right?"

"Right." I patted her and pulled away, not wanting this after all. I told her I'd drop by tonight, after Brian's in bed, and headed to the door.

"You okay?" she said.

"I'm fine. I'll see you later."

"Pick up a movie."

"All right."

"No John Wayne, though."

Out in the car I started the engine—and then I just sat there wondering what the hell to do with myself next, staring through the windshield at that sky I told you about: this great big milky gray empty blank nothing. And pretty soon, I'm not kidding, I felt like I was drifting into it—*turning* into it. Honest to God, I felt like I was disappearing. It scared the shit out of me. I drove back to the Palace.

"Chicken Little returns," Tommy announced, still the only one there.

I was actually glad to see him. I sat just a few stools away. The Cub game was still going, Cubs at bat. Tommy filled me in: "Tied in the thirteenth, two outs, runner on second, Grace at the plate. I'm gonna call you 'Chicklit' for short, how's that."

"Fine." Compared to other names he's had for me.

Larry brought me over an Old Style.

Grace tried to check his swing and sent a one-hopper back to the mound, Tommy shouting, "Asshole!"

I told Larry to bring my friend here another draft.

Tommy gave me a worried look. "How's your head?"

"Better," I told him.

My head wasn't so good the next morning, but not from any falling baseballs.

It was raining out, this dismal Sunday-morning drizzle, and I laid in bed trying to remember if I did anything last night to feel sorry about, besides forgetting my date with Karen.

I remembered the Palace getting loud and crowded, everyone coming up to me—even strangers—asking how's my head, with an amused little look in their eye.

I remembered talking to Redman for a while, getting one of his Indian warrior pep talks.

I remembered Tommy calling me "Chicklit."

Then I turned on my side and my eye fell on this framed photo I keep on the wall and I remembered telling somebody The Story. That's what Tommy calls it: The Story. It's true, though. One day when I was a little kid I played catch in Comiskey Park with White Sox second baseman Nellie Fox and afterwards we talked together. And sometimes when I get drunk I find somebody to tell it to. I wonder who I found last night. And I wonder what I told them.

The thing is, I've told it so many times in so many ways I don't remember what the real story is anymore. I know it happened, though. I've got the photograph: me and Nellie, outside the White Sox dugout. I'm wearing a Sox uniform, holding Nellie's huge club of a bat, and he's squatting with his arm around my waist. This is probably after we played catch—my glove's on the ground in front of us, with a ball. And then I definitely know we had a little chat together. Something like:

"So, Hank, how old are you?"

"I'm seven, Mr. Fox."

"Call me Nellie."

"Okay, Mr. Fox—I mean, Nellie!"

Nellie laughed.

"Y'know, you got a fine pair of infielder's hands there, Hank."

"Thank you, Nellie."

"What position do you like to play?"

"Second base, Nellie. Same as you."

"Attaboy. Y'know, you remind me of myself at your age."

"I do?"

"Yep. You got that same eagerness. That same hustle and heart."

"Gee . . ."

"Don't ever lose it, Hank. Just keep hustling. And who knows, maybe someday you'll take my job away."

"I wouldn't wanna do *that*, Nellie!"

Nellie laughed. "Hey, somebody's gonna take it someday, and I'd like to see a fella like you be the one."

I couldn't speak.

Nellie gave my waist a little squeeze. "Well, I better go take some batting practice."

I gave him his bat back.

"Just remember, Hank. Keep hustling."

I stood there watching him trot away, number 2 on his back.

Anyway, laying there in bed I couldn't remember killing or raping or robbing anyone last night, so I got up and made coffee.

I was on my second cup, reading some bullshit on the back of a Wheaties box, when the phone rang. I keep it in the bedroom, on the floor by the bed. I figured it was either Karen or else Gordie our team manager. They both had a reason to be pissed off at me.

"Hello?"

"Lingerman," he said.

"Gordie," I said.

"You wanna tell me about it?" he goes.

About leaving the game yesterday, he meant.

I said, "Nah."

"So you dropped a pop-up—so you go *home*? Without saying nothing? How's that make *me* look? I'm supposed to be the manager, you know? The guy at the wheel, the—"

"We win?"

"That's not the point, Lingerman. You're missing the fucking point. The point is, you don't *ever* go walking off like that without—"

I hung up.

It was too early on a Sunday morning and I was too hungover and anyway where's he get off talking to me like that, a twenty-one-year-old kid talking to me like that?

The phone rang again right away and I let it. And when it finally stopped ringing I just sat there on the edge of the bed realizing I had probably just cut myself from the team, that this was probably it for me and that it *should* be, and not just for the rest of the season but for the rest of my life because, let's face it, when the balls begin landing on your skull instead of in your glove . . .

I laid on my back and stared at the ceiling.

I tried to feel okay about this, thinking how lucky I've been, playing ball all these years: Little League, Babe Ruth League, Connie Mack League, a city semi-pro league, then all those years in the minors, ending up back here in this local adult league. A long and happy career. I thought of Lou Gehrig telling Yankee Stadium, "Today . . . I consider myself . . . the luckiest man . . . on the face of the earth." And he was *dying*. At least I wasn't dying. I had the whole rest of my life to go. Without baseball.

I pulled the sheet up over my head.

From all those years of long boring bus trips in the minors, I'm pretty good at sending myself to sleep, tired or not, and I didn't wake up until around four when the phone went off again. I could tell it was Karen this time, the way it kept on ringing, saying, *I know you're there . . . I know you're there . . .*

I sat up and yawned and stretched and rubbed my eyes and shook myself awake. Then I cleared my throat, picked up the phone and said, "Hello?"

"Where were you?"

"Just now?"

"Last night."

"Right. I was supposed to come over. The thing is . . ." But I didn't feel like making something up. Ever get like that? "Thing is, I just forgot," I said.

"Forgot," she said.

"Right."

Silence.

"Got drunk and just plain forgot," I said.

"That's swell, Hank. Can I ask you something?"

"All right."

"Are you at all interested in going on with this?"

"On with . . ."

"Us, Hank. With us. You and me."

"Sure I'm interested," I told her. "Of course I am."

Silence.

I knew she'd worked at the hospital today so I asked her how it went, to get off the subject of Us.

She didn't answer right away. Then she said, "Mr. Klausner died."

He was this old guy with cancer she sometimes took care of, washing him and helping him eat and so on. She liked him, how grouchy and brave he was.

I told her I was sorry. Then I wondered: "Did he say anything?"

She didn't understand the question.

I said, "You know, like . . . last words. Did he have anything to say?" I thought maybe he had some final thoughts about it all. Some advice maybe.

But she said he died early this morning, before she came on.

It sounded like she was crying a little, so I asked her if she wanted me to come over.

"I don't know . . ." she said.

I could tell she wanted me to talk her into it. But I didn't really want to come over. For one thing her kid, Brian, would be there. And anyway I just felt like staying in bed and listening to the goddam rain.

I said to her, "Well, give me a call if you decide you want some company, okay?"

She gave a sigh and said, "Go to hell, Hank."

"Well, hey . . ."

She hung up.

I sat there with the phone in my hand.

What a lousy thing to say to someone. You know? When you think about it? Go to hell. Go to the most horrible place you could possibly imagine.

I tried to imagine . . .

Maybe it wouldn't be anything real dramatic, like with flames and devils and such. Maybe hell was just a messy little apartment on a drizzly Sunday afternoon with a hangover and nothing to look forward to, forever.

A voice came on the phone, scaring me. It was the operator, telling me to hang up.

I did. Then I tried to snap out of it. I got up and made the bed. Then I picked up in the living room. Then I did the dishes. Then I cooked some vegetable soup—my own recipe, calling for one can of vegetable soup—and brought it into the living room, turned on the TV and watched a couple frames of a bowling match. But I still had such a headache I got up and changed the channel. It was too violent.

The Sox-Angels game on the West Coast was just getting under way, but I didn't want to think about baseball. I found a nature show about bees, with this quiet soothing narrator.

It turned out to be quite interesting. What struck me most about those bees, everyone in the whole group—the colony—had their job and did it constantly, non-stop, no time off till they died. Which on the one hand's a very tough life, for sure, but on the other hand you would never have days like this, sitting in front of the TV wondering what the fuck, I'm forty years old and what the fuck.

After the bees I got up and turned it off. Then I just stood there in the middle of the room with my hands in my bathrobe pockets . . . and made a decision.

I went to the bedroom and called Karen back. I got her machine: "Hi. We're not home right now. Please leave a message at the tone. Thank you."

I waited for the beep and said, "Hi. It's me. Hank. Listen. Let's get married. Right away. I think we should. All right? I'll be here if you wanna call. Okay? Thanks. Bye."

I was sitting on the edge of the bed breathing hard. You can't call back and erase those things.

I got up and started walking all over the apartment, telling myself what a wonderful person Karen was and what a lucky son of a bitch I would be, to be married to such a wonderful person. It didn't matter about how fat she'd got because she was such a wonderful person. And anyway, she could lose it. If she could put it on, she could take it off. She was already working on it. No problem there at all. And besides, who the hell was I, Jim Palmer? Not even close.

But there was something else. Her son, Brian. He'd be part of the package. And I'm sorry but I can't stand that kid. I've tried but I can't. Know what he says to her when he doesn't get his way? "Thanks a lot, Mom. It's real nice to be loved." That kind of kid. And he's only ten. He'd be there for another ten years, while Karen just kept getting fatter . . .

I called her back.

"Hi. We're not home right now . . ."

I hung up. I grabbed my hair. *What to do?*

I got dressed and drove to the Palace.

It was pretty crowded for a Sunday night. The Sox-Angels game was on, everyone watching except Tommy, who won't even *glance* at the White Sox.

I got drunk. And I got nasty. I started sounding off about these ballplayers today, these arrogant, millionaire, one-handing, hotdogging, pay-for-my-autograph punks, with their agents and their wrist bands and their batting gloves and their butt-hugging pants and their fucking *jewelry*, for Chrissake, and what the hell ever happened to *real* ballplayers? Guys like Nellie Fox. Now *there* was a goddam *ballplayer* . . .

And when some burly jerk I never saw before said, "Ah, shut up, old man," I went over to his stool.

I asked him, "What did you say to me?" Asked him politely, you know? Like I really didn't hear him. Like what I *thought* I heard just had to be wrong.

He leaned towards my face and told me very carefully, "I said shut . . . the fuck . . . up . . . old . . . man."

I shoved the son of a bitch off his stool.

He got up and beat the shit out of me.

I ended up under the pool table. And you know what I thought about, lying there? Those bees. *They* wouldn't be here, I thought.

2. I made it to work the next morning. I almost always do. I'm a mechanic at Whitey's Sunoco, this garage in town my dad used to own. He wanted to sell it to me but I didn't want the headache and anyway I was still hanging on in the minors. He wanted me to quit hanging on but I wouldn't, so he ended up selling it to his mechanic, George Turner, great big black guy about fifty now. My dad's only condition was that George keep the name of the place, for old times' sake. So that's why it's still called Whitey's. Which is kind of funny, although George doesn't think so.

He asked me about my face—it was a little swelled up and blue on one side from last night.

I told him I got hit by a pitch in Saturday's game.

"Is that right?"

I nodded, pouring some coffee.

He said, "Now, see, the way *I* heard it, you got hit on *top* the head."

Jesus H. Christ.

"Yeah, well . . . that was a few innings earlier."

He shook his head. "Dangerous damn game, ain't it."

"Sometimes. Listen, what've we got today?"

He told me, and I went to work, starting with a brake problem on an '87 Tercel, while helping out with the pumps until

Darryl got in. The Tercel took me all the way through noon, and then without stopping for lunch I started replacing an exhaust system on a Jeep Cherokee, and after that I inspected somebody's new '91 Accord, then spent the rest of the day installing a new starter in a Chevy pickup. I didn't come back to myself until I knocked off at four.

This job is good that way.

I was showered and getting into clean clothes when the phone rang. Karen, I figured. Probably already picked out her gown and the reception hall. I let it ring. Better to just go over there and explain in person. I wasn't in any hurry, though, so I walked. It's only about a mile.

Boy, I'll tell you something, this town's really starting to lose its looks. It's a suburb from the fifties. My folks moved here from the South Side—fled here, like all the other white people were doing—and now it's finally getting that sad, grimy, edge-of-the-city look. Plus, the blacks have caught up, more and more moving in every day. Seeing them around really gives it a city look.

I walked past the park. A few little kids were in the playground section. And, as usual, nobody at all was on the ball diamond.

That always gets to me, when I see nobody out there. The backstop is still in good shape and the town still cuts the grass. The infield dirt and home plate area could use a good raking, but otherwise the field's as good as ever. But you never see anyone using it.

Christ, we used to be out there first thing every morning, the grass still a little wet. I'd ride up on my bike, my glove hanging from the handle bars, and guys would be playing catch, playing pepper, hitting flyballs, sitting on the picnic bench trading cards. Tommy would be there, always arguing about his sad old Cubs and how if they were in the *American* League they'd be kicking everybody's ass. Then, soon as we had enough guys, two of us would flip a bat to pick sides and we'd figure out positions. Being Nellie Fox, I always took second base. Tommy would climb on top of the backstop to do the play-by-play broadcast, brought to you by Hamm's, the beer refreshing, from the land of sky-blue waters. We'd wait for him to shout, loud as he could, "Plaaay baaawwwll!" And then we'd play. And I mean to the hilt. And play all damn day.

It saddens me to see nobody out there now. It really does. And disgusts me, too.

Karen's got a nice big solid brick house from her ex. About four years ago he fell for a client at his sue-their-ass law firm, a German woman, and told Karen to take it all— house, car and kid—*just let me go*. So she did, and he went to live with his fraulein. But she threw him out after only a month, for sloppiness—wet towels on the bathroom floor, things like that. Near the end, she actually called Karen for advice on how to get him to pick up after himself. Karen told her she always used a good stick on him.

I knocked at the back door and walked in. She was in the kitchen doing dishes in a sweat suit, losing an ounce or two.

"Jesus, what happened?" she goes, when she saw my face, which was still swelled-up a bit.

"Little accident at work," I told her.

She wiped her hands on a dish towel and came up for a close examination, wanting to know if it hurts, and how about an ice pack.

I told her I'm fine, thinking maybe I should go ahead and marry this nice lady. In fact, I told her to finish washing the dishes and I'll dry, figuring that would put me over the top. Doing dishes together always makes me feel like marrying her.

But she said, "No. Let's go sit in the living room."

"You're gonna lose all your suds."

"I'll get over it."

Walking down the hall past Brian's room I could hear all kinds of video game mayhem going on in there. All those kids missing from the ball field, this was what they were doing.

We sat on the couch with some distance between us. She went right to the point. "I got your message," she said, nodding at the phone on the coffee table.

I nodded at it, too. Then we just sat there looking at the damn thing.

She told me she didn't get back last night until around nine, after taking Brian to a movie.

I asked her what movie she saw. Just stalling.

"*Free Willy*."

"About the dolphin?"

"Whale."

"How was it?"

"Sweet. Brian hated it. Or said he did. I tried calling you every half hour until almost—"

"Know what *I* liked when I was a kid but wouldn't admit? Peter Pan. Not the cartoon but the real thing. Ever see it? I'll tell you something, the guy who played Captain—"

"Where'd you go last night?"

"The bar. I was watching the Sox game."

She looked amazed. "I don't believe you."

"Why would I lie?"

"I mean, I can't believe you would leave me a message like that and then go out and watch the *ball*game. Do you remember saying you'd be home if I wanted to call? Do you remember *any* of it? Or were you drunk?"

"I wasn't drunk. I called *before* I left."

"So, do you remember what you said, Hank? What you asked me?"

"'*Course* I remember. Basically what I said was, we should probably begin to start thinking a little bit about the future and the possibility of someday getting . . . you know . . . married, when the time is right, and if you wanted to discuss it a little more I'd be home for a while. Now, I don't know what you might have read into it, Karen, but that was the basic message."

She stabbed a button on the phone in front of her and this zombie voice said, "I will . . . replay . . . message." The tape whirred.

"Karen," I said—in a whisper, for some reason—"I don't wanna hear—"

"Shh."

The thing beeped and then I heard my stupid fucking self saying, "Hi. It's me. Hank. Listen. Let's get married. Right away. I think we should. All right? I'll be here if you wanna call. Okay? Thanks. Bye."

She poked another button and the zombie said, "I will . . . save . . . message."

She sat there looking at me. "My answer is yes, Hank."

I looked down at my shoes. I was sweating this clammy kind of sweat I get and there was ice in the pit of my stomach and a voice in my head hollering, *Run!*

But I didn't. And all of a sudden I was okay. I was calm. I was caught, I had to surrender, and I felt this great relief. I looked at her, my bride-to-be.

But before I could speak, something flew just over the top of my head and broke against the television screen, slid down and dropped on the carpet—a raw egg.

I turned around but he was gone, around the corner and back to his room, slamming the door, Karen up and after him.

I sat there listening while she banged on his locked door and told him to open it, to come out here right now and tell Hank you're sorry. "Brian!" she yelled, and banged some more. "Brian, answer me, dammit!"

I got up and walked across the room and out the door.

Soon as I stepped in the Palace, Jerry started shouting, "Out! I told you! One week!"—meaning one week suspension, for fighting.

I said, "Fine. Fuck it," and walked out again. I had beer at home.

Plus crackers and cream cheese and Spanish olives. I set it all on the coffee table and found another nature show. This one was about elephants, the plight of the elephant . . .

Christ, you know what I would do to those goddam ivory poachers? You know what I would do to those sonofabitches?

I don't know what I would do. Probably nothing. Who cares?

Over our coffee this morning before we got started, George said his wife was looking for something in the attic yesterday and found a scorecard from a 1953 Sox-Indians game that says in pen, *To George, Good wishes, Minnie Minoso.*

I told him that's really something to have, and it is.

I've never told him The Story—about playing catch with Nellie Fox—and I thought about telling him now, except I didn't feel like topping him, you know? And anyway I really just wanted to start working. Like I mentioned before, fixing cars is a good way to put everything in your head on hold for a while. Plus, you feel like you're at least fixing *some*thing.

But George poured us both another cup and started going on about Minoso, calling him "my man," saying how he belongs in the Hall of Fame, which I guess you could make a case for. But then he said something stupid. He said Minoso was by far the best Sox player of the fifties.

I said, "George, come on."

"Where we going? Name somebody better."

"You remember Nellie Fox?"

"Sure do. Little sawed-off man, chewed tobacco, liked to bunt a lot. What about him?"

I held my temper. I asked him, just for starters, if his man ever won the League's Most Valuable Player Award, which Fox received in '59.

George said he doubted if Minoso won *any* damn awards, being a black player back in those days.

I gave a sigh and said, "Here we go."

That was a mistake.

George stood there with his head tilted, kind of studying me. "Where we going now?" he said, very calm and quiet and scary.

I said we weren't going anywhere, standing around arguing about old-time ballplayers at seven-thirty in the morning, for Christ sake, and walked off into the car bay.

It didn't work. He followed me.

I went over to a Mazda I'd been working on yesterday and started opening the hood, but he put his hand on it.

I stood there looking at those fingers, thinking what a big fist they would make. "All right, look, I'm sorry," I said. "Okay?" I didn't feel like getting my ass kicked twice in three days. "I shouldn't have said that and I apologize, all right?"

All he did was shake his head, looking disgusted. Then he muttered, "Whitey Junior," and walked off.

That didn't hurt. Why should it? Whitey's my race and Whitey's my dad.

But it did hurt. I felt like George was disappointed in me. Like he had thought I was something better than Whitey Junior.

I stayed in again that night and watched a bunch of sitcoms in a row. I started to laugh out loud at something Norm said on *Cheers* but stifled it. I don't like to hear myself sitting there all alone laughing at the television. You know?

Meanwhile I kept listening for the phone, expecting Karen to call. And by eight-thirty I couldn't stand it anymore and rang her up and apologized for my cowardly behavior. That's how I put it: my cowardly behavior. And I invited her out to dinner tomorrow night, Brian included, to Antonio's, the best restaurant in town, in fact the *only* one in town.

She said, "No, I'm sorry."

Just like that.

I waited for more. But there wasn't any.

I said, "Okay. Well . . ."

"Goodbye, Hank," she said, and hung up.

Which seemed kind of final. Very final, in fact.

I sat there on the edge of the bed waiting to see how I felt about that.

I'd like to say that all of a sudden my heart cracked right in half and I called her back and words came pouring out of my cracked-open heart, words of love and sorrow and devotion, and Karen said similar things, and then I told her to put Brian on and I promised that boy I would try my best to be a father to him and maybe someday, who knows, he would call me Dad, and Brian said to me, *Okay . . . Dad.*

But none of that happened.

I've had love and sorrow, though. But not for a long time. Not since Wendy. And that was, Jesus, ten years ago.

Wendy Pelletier, from Beeville, Texas, just forty miles north of the Rio Grande. I was playing single-A ball down there with the Beeville Bees. And I just thought of something interesting. Remember those bees on TV I told you about? Well, that's the kind of ball club we had, everybody doing their job, working together for the good of the team—or the colony, you could say. See, almost all of us were past the age where we could still hope for a shot at the Show, so we weren't just out for ourselves, hoping to move up. We knew we weren't going anywhere. We were just down there playing ball under that hot, hot sun for 600 dollars a month because that's what we wanted to be doing.

And I'll tell you something. We were good. Not a lot of speed or power or even much pitching, but solid glove men all, and like I said, we were a bee hive. We would bunt, hit-and-run, delay steal, out-think and out-hustle our way past teams with twice the talent. Just a good, tough, scrappy, fundamental, old-fashioned type ball club. A team Nellie Fox would have enjoyed playing on.

Ugly uniforms, though. Black and yellow. Bees, you see.

Anyway, you talk about fans. These people couldn't do enough for us. I don't think I paid for a meal all summer. We even got gifts from local store owners. I still have a sharp-looking three-piece suit I got for a diving, game-saving catch I made on a shallow fly to right—which *was* a hell of a catch.

And girls. They liked us. All of us. I met Wendy the first week of the season. It was at a barbecue the team owner gave at his ranch outside of town, with steers and cows and horses, the whole Bonanza bit, and he ordered an entire Budweiser truck, everybody sitting around with steaks and beer. I didn't used to drink during the season back then and I've never cared for steak so I was standing there under a tree with a plate of potato salad, and this sweet-faced girl in a halter top and cut-offs comes walking up on her long brown legs and says in this sexy Texan drawl, "Hi, Hank! That was a real nice bunt you made today!"

And I said, "Well, *thank* you."

Then all that summer it was just baseball and Wendy.

But then the season ended and we had to say goodbye. We promised to write, and we did. She wrote first, saying how much she missed me, and I wrote back saying how much I missed *her*. Then a week later, without even hearing from her again, she was standing at my door holding a big suitcase and a bird cage with her parakeet Tina in it. Tina looked pretty ragged but Wendy looked great.

"Hi, Hank!" she said.

A week after that we got married at the Town Hall.

And about a month or so after that we were driving somewhere and I happened to notice she was sitting there crying, quietly. I asked her what's the matter but she wouldn't say. So I pulled off into the breakdown lane and asked her again. And she finally said through her tears, "I'm just . . . so . . . *bored*." Then she started crying really hard.

And that was it for me and Wendy. She went back to Beeville with Tina and we worked out the divorce through the mail.

I was in pretty bad shape for a while. She was so damn sweet and pretty. She really was.

I ended up getting a dog for some company, mostly just to tell him all about how bad I felt. One of those little wiener dogs. Scooter, I called him. But then he took off on me, too. Probably for the same reason Wendy did.

After getting off the phone with Karen I was stuck with nothing to do but more TV, and sometimes watching a lot of TV makes me feel like I have no life—or reminds me that I don't. So I called my dad down in Arizona.

"Hello. Who's this?" That's how he answers the phone.

I said, "Hey, Whitey."

"Well, for Chrissake," he goes, meaning it's about time I called.

I asked him how he's doing and stretched out on the bed on my back. He never used to be a talker, especially on the phone, but now, Jesus, he's worse than my mom was, and she was amazing.

He started out with the beautiful weather . . .

The way he ended up down there, I was playing in Tempe with a team in the Dodgers organization the summer my mom died—from emphysema—and about a month later he flew down for a visit, probably running away from nights like this one I'm having, and fell in love with the palm trees and swimming pools and the horrible heat and the women—hell, yes—and within a year he'd sold the house and the station and was living in one of those retirement communities in Scottsdale, happy as a lizard, which he kind of looks like anyway.

After the weather report he told me all about a long walk he took through the desert this morning with his beautiful sexy young Mexican girlfriend Carlotta, and how he handled a rattlesnake that suddenly appeared in their path, quickly pulling Carlotta behind him and then just staring it down, just staring the slimy sonofabitch down until it turned and went slinking away, and Carlotta called him something in Mexican which means my wonderful man who knows no fear.

I was going to ask him about knowing Mexican, just to see how he handled *that*—but the thing is, you can hear in his voice he's happy down there, and maybe there *is* a Carlotta, even if she's not all that beautiful and young and sexy, so I just kept saying "No shit" and "Wow" and "You're kidding."

Then he goes, "I don't think I better tell you the rest of what happened," and gives this dirty-old-man laugh.

Then he says, "So. Anyway. What's new with you?"

"Not much."

"Still with the Chicago White Sox?"

That's his little joke about me being on this rinky-dink local team. Thing is, he's still resentful as hell that I kept hanging on in the minors instead of taking over the station.

I told him, "Actually, no. I sort of quit."

"About time, for Chrissake."

"Why do you say that?"

"Well, Jesus, Hank. What're you now, almost forty?"

"I *am* forty. But so what?"

"You're forty?" he goes. "You're forty years old?"

"That's right," I said, "but I'll tell you something, I can still outplay these punks any goddam day of the week."

"Don't swear at me, Hank."

"I'm not. I'm just saying, that's all. I'm just saying."

"Take it easy, boy."

"I am."

"How's the station doing?"

"The station's fine."

"How's Bwana?"—meaning George, the joke being here's this black guy who's my boss instead of the other way around, which is supposed to bother me.

I told him George was fine.

"And that lady friend of yours, with the little boy. What's her name? Carol?"

"Karen. She's fine, too." I didn't feel like going into that.

"Any particular *plans* I should know about?"

He wants me to get married and give him a grandson and maybe *he'll* take over the station. He's told me that.

I said, "No. No plans."

He gave a big sigh and didn't say anything. I figured what was next and I was right.

"Your mother came to see me last night," he said.

"How's she doing."

"Fine, except . . . well, she's awful worried about you, Hank."

"Is that right."

"Awfully concerned. She says you have no focus. No direction. And she can't rest, you see. The poor thing can't rest until she sees you getting your life into some kind of . . . well . . ."

"Shape?"

"That's right. I think that's the very word she used."

I hate when he lays this on me, about my mom not being able to rest.

"You see, Hank—"

"Hey, Dad, can I ask you something?"

"What is it."

"I was just wondering. When Mom comes to see you? What's she *look* like?"

"What's she look like?"

"Right."

"What the hell you *think* she looks like. She looks like your mother."

"Yeah but I mean is she, you know, wearing *wings*, for example?"

"What're you, a little kid?"

"I'm just wondering. Like last night. What was she wearing? I'm just curious."

"Last night?"

"Yeah."

"As a matter of fact, she was wearing her mumu. Her mumu and her slippers."

I laughed. I couldn't help it.

"And that's funny?" he said. "Your dead mother? That's something to laugh about?"

"I'm sorry," I said. Making it three different people I'd apologized to that day.

"I don't *know* about you, Hank. I really don't."

"Yeah, well . . . me neither."

We didn't say anything for a moment. I wanted to get the hell off now and was trying to think how. Then he asked me, "What's the weather like? Raining?"

"Buckets."

It wasn't raining at all but he likes to hear that, since it's always so nice and sunny down there.

"Got your car windows up?"

"Oh Christ, I forgot," I told him.

"Nice going."

"I better go. Good talking to you, Dad. Take care of yourself."

"Oh, I will."

I walked around the apartment for a while. Then I turned on the goddam TV again.

3. After George decided I was Whitey Junior he didn't speak to me all that day and half the next except when necessary and then mostly through his son-in-law Darryl who helps out with the pumps and the register.

You could feel this big hot silence coming off him.

And I have to admit, by the middle of Day Two it was getting to me a little. But I'd already apologized, so what the hell else did he want me to do, kiss his black ass? Fuck that.

But then he came over.

I'd been chewing a lot of tobacco—it calms me down—and was stuffing my face with a fresh wad over by the tool corner, when he comes strolling up, pointing at me, going, "Nellie Fox."

I said, "Mm?"

"That's how come you stick that shit in your mouth, ain't it."

To be like my hero Nellie Fox, he meant. Which was maybe why I started out chewing, but after twenty years I like to think of it as my own bad habit. But I couldn't talk while I was working the wad into my cheek, so all I did was shrug like an idiot, which I guess I am.

He lit a cigarette and put his big-booted foot up on the work bench. "Old Nellie Fox," he said. "So that was *your* man, huh?"

I nodded.

"You had Nellie and I had Minnie."

I nodded.

"Sounds like a couple girlfriends we had, don't it?" he said.

I laughed—and wiped off my chin.

He gave a long sigh and said it sure didn't seem like no thirty, thirty-five years ago.

I shook my head.

He said it wouldn't surprise him, though, if Minnie was still in the game somewhere, Mexico or Cuba, some place like that.

I spat in a little styrofoam cup and said it wouldn't surprise me either. And it wouldn't. Good old Minnie.

"So what's your man up to these days?" he asked.

"Not much. He's dead," I told him. "Nineteen seventy-five."

"Is that right? What got him?"

"Cancer."

George nodded. "Well, he was a fine ballplayer, no doubt about that."

I corrected him, "A great ballplayer."

"Think so?"

"I do. Yes."

"Well . . . you might be right."

That was acceptable.

"Trouble is," he added, "that's a very strong word, 'great.' Very strong word."

"I think it fits."

"Like I said, you might be right."

"But you don't think so."

"Actually, no, I'm afraid I don't."

"But you think it fits Minoso."

"Like a glove. And I'll tell you why," he said, his boot on the bench, leaning towards me, all set to start ticking off a list of reasons on his big thick fingers.

But I put up my hand and told him, "That's all right."

I figured, what the hell, it's good he liked Minnie Minoso. Minnie was a good hero to have. A shame he didn't know enough to appreciate Fox more, but I said to him, "You had Minnie and I had Nellie."

"There you go," he said, and took his boot off the bench. "There you go."

We went back to work.

December 1, 1975, to be exact. I remember the headline in the Sun-Times:

Sox Favorite Nellie Fox Dies

He was only forty-seven. I didn't even know he was sick. There was this long letter I was always going to write him.

A few months later I visited his grave. I was on my way down to Raleigh, North Carolina, for my second year with a Tigers rookie league team and detoured to St. Thomas, Pennsylvania, where he was born and buried. A pretty little town, hills and apple orchards all around it. I pulled into a little two-pump gas station, got out and said, "Hi!" to an old guy standing in the doorway.

He nodded.

I walked up and asked him if he happened to know where Nellie Fox was laid to rest. I didn't want to say "buried."

"Where he's what?" The guy's name was Stan, according to his shirt pocket.

"Where his grave is," I said.

He looked behind me, at the Illinois plates. "From Chicago?" he asked.

"Near there."

He nodded, acting just like someone in a movie who's supposed to be an old, hicktown gas station attendant. Then, from the same movie: "You a reporter?"

"No," I said, trying to think what I was.

"Just a fan, huh?"

"I guess."

"And you came all the way here so you could look at his grave?"

I shrugged. I felt foolish.

Stan did some more nodding. All he needed was a toothpick. Then he said, "Well, I s'pose old Pug wouldn't mind a visitor."

"Pug?" I said. "Was that his nickname? Pug?"

He pointed up the street. "Stay on this to the next light. Make a left . . ."

Stan wasn't sure where the grave was located, but the cemetery turned out to be a small one, as they go, so I just parked near the entrance and went looking for him. It was still early morning, cold and misty.

As I walked around I started thinking back.

We always got there early, me and my dad, a good hour before game time, box seats right behind the first base dugout, courtesy of Sparky Collins, the Sox equipment manager, who lived around here and brought his car to Whitey's. It was through Sparky I got to play catch with Nellie, by the way. Anyway, my dad would take off his shirt and drink beer and work on the horses in his scratch sheet and I'd watch the players taking infield and batting practice. And it was always Nellie I kept my eye on. Being a runt myself, I liked how little he was, and the way his cheek bulged out from the wad of chaw, and this happiness he seemed to have out there, punching the pocket of his glove, this dinky little glove about the size of mine, and how he'd get all the way down on a grounder, down to one knee sometimes, grabbing up the ball with both hands, then springing to his feet and firing it side-arm to the bag, squinting over his arm as he followed through. I worked on that in our own games down at the park, with a wad of licorice in my cheek. And I worked on the way he batted: from the left side, holding my hands a good inch and a half up the handle and never trying for distance, just punching the ball, shooting it through the infield, or dropping a dead little bunt down the line and racing like crazy to first . . .

I saw this headstone with just the word FOX, and walked around to the other side of it.

It was him.

FOR NELLIE TO LIVE IN THE HEARTS OF THOSE WHO REMAIN, it said. Then all the way down the stone it listed his career statistics and highlights, like the back of a giant baseball card. And at the end it said, WELL DONE.

I stood there for a long time wanting to say something. How I felt about him. But I kept hearing Stan back at the gas station calling him "Pug." Maybe that was what everyone called him, everyone who knew him, and here I'd never even heard it before. And how could I? Being just a fan. Some goofy idolizer who drove all the way here and then couldn't think of anything to say to him. I felt foolish, and cold and wet.

I walked back to the car.

But after I was out of town and on the turnpike again, heading towards another baseball season, I started thinking: I knew something about Nellie that they didn't know. Something important. I knew how he felt playing ball the way he'd played it. That happiness. Stan didn't know anything about that. None of them did. That was something between me and Nellie.

All day long today, at work and then at home, I thought about calling Gordie and apologizing for leaving the game Saturday, and also for hanging up on him when he called. Then I would ask him to let me stay on the team—beg him, if that's what it took. And at one point, around six- thirty, I got as far as picking up the phone. But then I remembered everyone's reaction when that ball fell on my head: nobody laughing or saying a word or even looking at me. And I put the phone back down.

Then it got to be seven-thirty, a beautiful evening for a ball game, and they'd be just starting. But instead of me out there at second base there'd be someone else, probably Dunbar, who doesn't even *like* second base . . .

I left the apartment and went driving around. I still had a couple days left on my suspension from the Palace so I went out to this bar near the mall, called The Purple Angel. But pulling into the lot I could hear the music pounding away in there and I felt too old. So I drove back to town and ended up stopping at Antonio's, in the little empty lounge off the restaurant.

Tony noticed me right away and came hurrying in, in his white tuxedo with a red sash and carnation and his shiny black hair. "Hey, Stromboli!" That's what he calls me. I'm not sure what it means. Nothing bad, I don't think. We've been friends all the way back to grade school.

Back then he had this amazing thing he could do. He could turn a complete somersault just standing there, like a little monkey. So we would tell everyone I could do judo, and to prove it I would grab his wrist and give his arm a quick twist and he'd flip right over. It kept a lot of people from messing with me. Which was good because, like I mentioned, I was a runt.

He drew me an Old Style and said he'd heard from Officer Phil about the fight in the Palace Sunday night. "Guess that guy won't ever fuck with *you* again, huh?"

"Not likely."

"Give him the old judo flip?"

"All over the place."

He laughed. "That's my Stromboli."

He was talking in his regular voice. When he walks around the restaurant dropping in at tables, he puts on this Italian accent. Everyone knows it's bogus but he does it anyway. For atmosphere, I guess.

He stood there watching me take a drink. Then he said, "What's the matter, man?"

"Nothing." I wiped my mouth. "Why?"

"I don't know. You look lost."

I looked in the mirror behind the bottles. It was hard to tell. But maybe that was part of being lost.

"You still with that Karen chick?"

"I don't know. I don't think so."

"What the fuck kinda answer is that?"

I shrugged.

He shook his head at me. "Go out there and get some pussy, Stromboli. That's what you need."

"All right."

"No, for real. Just make sure you don't end up like this guy I know. I ever tell you about him?"

Tony's always got a new joke about some guy out looking for pussy, and it's always long and complicated as hell. I sipped my beer and waited it out.

He finally got to the punch line: "And he says to the bitch, he goes, 'Weell, didn't taste *too* bad.'"

I nodded. "That's funny. I like that." I got up and put two dollars on the bar, one for the beer and one for the joke.

Tony tried again, "'Didn't taste *too* bad.'"

"That's a good one."

"You're supposed to laugh, Stromboli."

"I will, later."

Driving home I saw the lights—and I couldn't help it, I turned down Broad to Heenan Park. I pulled in along the left field line, past the bleachers, near Officer Phil's car.

We—or I should say *they*—were in the field, Redman out on the mound. Even at this distance I could hear Gordie in the dugout screaming at the umps over something. And there was Dunbar out at second base, out at my spot, with that flap of curly yellow locks out the back of his cap and his neon wrist bands and his white shoes and that big long stupid fucking glove he uses.

Officer Phil hollered from his car, "Hey, Lingerman! What'd you do, hang it up?"

"Yeah," I said, my voice cracking in half.

I got the hell out of there.

One good thing. When I got home and turned on the TV it was just starting: *Rio Bravo*, starring John Wayne, Dean Martin, and Angie Dickinson as Feathers.

The legs on that woman.

Then afterwards I went to bed and instead of thinking about baseball I thought about making love to Angie Dickinson, real, real slow.

"Oh, Hank," she goes. "Oh, you big sweet man."

"Oh, Feathers."

The phone rang.

It was Gordie, wanting to know where the hell I was tonight.

George asked me this morning to please stop singing, at least so loud, even though I was doing all Stevie Wonder songs.

I like Stevie Wonder. I don't like to see him singing, though, tossing his head around like he does. He's blind, you know.

Anyway, I lowered the volume.

Which is pretty ridiculous, singing at all. I mean, here I am, a guy who's played pro ball—not the Bigs, but getting paid, so that's pro—and here I am singing away at seven-thirty in the morning because I'm back on some team in a local, two-games-a-week league you pay *them* to play in.

But see, it's still baseball. And last night on the phone Gordie told me to come back. He said he only had nine guys last night including Brownie who's atrocious and then Mueller sprained his ankle so Gordie had to put himself in and he's worse than Brownie. So it wasn't like a great compliment but still he was saying they need me, especially Saturday since Dunbar's not coming. So I was singing. Quietly, though.

The day went pretty quick, I got a lot done, and was home in the shower singing as loud as I wanted, doing a very nice job with "You Are the Sunshine of My Life," when all of a sudden, right in the middle of the song, standing there with my arms spread, my good mood ran out of gas and I was back on empty. I finished washing myself and got out.

Then I just stood there dripping wet, holding the towel, trying to think, trying to figure out what the hell was missing, what I really deep down wanted—like maybe even God or something, you know?

I had this roomie for a while when I was playing down in Tempe, guy named Sid Vansickle, a very tall, bony, hard-throwing right-hander, serious heat but only so-so control. Anyway, Sid was very tight with Jesus. Whenever he won a game he'd say the Lord was with him out there. And if he lost? Well, that was the Lord's will too. Either way, he was happy, about the happiest guy I ever knew. He was absolutely sure he was on his way to Heaven, so why get upset over things down here? It turned out the Lord wanted him to lose five games in a row while piling up an earned-run average of something like 6.5, and he got his pink slip. But he didn't mind. The Lord had other plans for him, that's all. God wanted him to go into real-estate management.

Anyway, the point is, I wouldn't mind having God, not a bit. Then every time I noticed another one of these goddam gray hairs in the mirror, instead of having to think about turning old and slow and feeble and worthless, I'd think about being that much closer to Heaven, where I'll be constantly absolutely happy forever—and meanwhile be happy as hell just knowing that's where I'm headed.

Pretty good deal.

So why not get down on my knees right there in the bathroom and pledge my soul to Our Lord and Savior Jesus Christ the Son of God, as Sid would put it.

Really. Why not?

I let my knees go a little soft, trying it out. Then I got all the way down on my right knee, like I sometimes do on a tough grounder.

But then I remembered something. I remembered how much I despised that fucking guy—Sid, not Jesus. I always felt like he was nothing but a kiss-ass. Because that's really what he was, you know? I mean, a kiss-ass is a kiss-ass, whether it's God's ass or anyone else's. And I'm not kissing anybody's ass. Not yet, anyway. I got off my knee and finished drying myself.

I knew what I *really* needed, for tonight at least. Tony was right. I shaved and afterwards slapped on some Old Spice. Lots of it.

4. The Purple Angel is this dance bar out by the mall, five dollars just to walk in the door, this being a very special, very classy place, with purple carpeting, purple pillars around the dance floor, the bartenders in purple vests and bow ties, the waitresses in purple tights with little gauzy wings on their backs and a drop-dead look in their eye.

Five fucking dollars.

I was leaning against one of those very special pillars, with a glass and a pitcher of Old Style (saves trips to the bar), watching the animals out on the dance floor, thinking to myself what a trashy generation of young people this country has on its hands. You should see them out there. They might as well just start fucking right there on the floor. It's not just disgusting, it's depressing. But I guess what's even more disgusting and depressing is me standing there watching them with a Louisville Slugger in my pants.

"*Hey!*" somebody next to me yelled.

It was this short little chick holding out her empty glass.

So I filled it from my pitcher, what the hell.

"*Thanks!*" she yelled, which you had to do in there.

I nodded. At least she said thanks.

"*What's your name?*" she yelled.

"*Hank!*" I yelled.

I knew she was waiting for me to ask what *her* name was, but I looked off towards the dance floor again, not wanting to get something started. She wasn't bad-looking—in fact she was kind of cute, except for one thing: this little ring in her nose. And I'm sorry but I don't talk to people with a ring in their nose. You have to draw the line somewhere.

"*My name's Mary!*" she yelled. "*Wanna dance?*"

I shook my head, no, without looking at her.

"*Come on!*"

I looked at her and she jerked her head towards the dance floor.

Pushy little thing.

And just then a new song came on and guess who it was. Stevie Wonder. "I Just Called to Say I Love You." Such a great song.

So I nodded Okay.

Right away she held up a finger for me to wait a second while she finished off her beer in one long drink. I didn't know what to do with my pitcher and glass and stood there looking around but she took them and put them on the floor against the pillar and grabbed my hand and led me out there.

I can't dance worth a damn, especially separately, so I was glad when she put her arms around me, except I don't agree with this total-embrace, dry-humping style of dancing, not in public anyway, for Christ sake, so I managed to get her hand in mine, and with my other hand at her little waist we moved around together very enjoyably in the tiny bit of room we had, and I quit thinking about that ring in her nose and being probably twice her age.

Then, when the song ended, she looked up and gave me a smile. It was the damndest thing. Just gave me this big old smile. And without even thinking, I gave her a little kiss on the forehead.

Then right away another song, a fast one, and before I could say anything she was dancing like mad in front of me. So what could I do, except my best, which is pitiful.

The song finally ended and she grabbed my hand and led me off the floor. My beer pitcher was still there but some sonofabitch had drank it all up. So I gave her a ten for a refill and she took the pitcher and headed into the crowd towards the bar while I waited by the pillar.

Well, she didn't come back and didn't come back and I kept getting more and more pissed off, thinking I should have known. I mean, let's face it, people these days are absolute total fucking garbage. The whole human race is sliding straight down the toilet. I mean, *look* at these people . . .

Then I saw her come out through the crowd. She was holding up the pitcher in both hands like a trophy, with that big old smile.

She tried everything she could. She even danced around the bed for me, nice and slow. And she had a sweet little body on her. But it was no go. It wasn't because I was drunk, because I wasn't.

She was nice about it, though. "How's it going?" she asked. She was facing the wall, hands on her head, swinging her pretty little butt.

"I'm sorry," I said to her for the hundredth time.

She kept dancing, though, enjoying herself. "Who's the picture?" she asked.

"What?"

"This kid with the baseball guy."

"Me and Nellie Fox."

"That's you? The kid?"

"Yes." I was staring at the ceiling now.

"Fat-faced little shit, weren't you."

"I guess."

"Was this guy a real baseball player?"

"Yes."

"Any good?"

I told her: "Most Valuable Player Award, 1959. Four Gold Glove Awards. Most consecutive games without striking out. Twelve All-Star appearances . . ."

She jumped back into bed. "He musta been really good," she said, and put her arms around me.

Strange little chick.

I said, "He was. He was great."

"He musta been your hero."

"He was, yes."

"I bet you played just like him."

I looked at her. "I try to."

"You still play baseball?"

I nodded.

"I bet you're good," she said in my ear.

"Well . . ."

"I bet you're really good," she whispered in my ear.

"I was."

"I bet you still are. I bet you're the best. The most valuable player," she whispered, right into my ear.

"Think so?"

"I can tell," she said, and put her little hand around my cock, which was doing much better now. "I can *tell.*"

"Can you?" I said.

"Oh, yeah."

"Can you?" I said, in kind of a state now.

She climbed aboard. "Oh, yes," she said.

"Really?"

"Oh, *yes*."

"I forgot your name!"

"Mary!"

"I'm Hank!"

"Hi!"

"Hi!"

In the middle of the night she started kicking me.

"Stop," I told her.

She started punching me.

"Hey, *stop*."

She sat up in the dark. "Shit, where am I?"

"You're with me," I told her, sitting up too. "I'm Hank. Remember?" I put my arm around her shoulder.

She shrugged it off. "Stuffy in here," she said, and laid back down.

I laid down too.

She turned the other way.

I put my hand on her hip. "Goodnight, Mary."

"'night."

When the alarm went off at 6:30 I killed it as quick as I could. She stirred a little but didn't wake up. I went and used the bathroom, came back and very quietly got dressed. She stayed asleep. I sat on the edge of the bed and watched her for a minute. She was curled up in the sheet, her mouth a little open, a strip of hair pasted on her forehead like she'd been sweating. That silly ring in her nose. I leaned down and kissed her cheek. She drew a long breath but went on sleeping. I left for work.

Around eleven, I called. It kept ringing away. I gave it three more rings . . . two . . . one . . .

"Hello?"—in her scratchy little voice.

I tried not to show anything. "Hi. It's me. Hank."

She didn't respond.

"From last night. The guy who lives there," I explained.

"Oh. Hi."

"Hi. Listen, there's food in the fridge. Some cold cuts and lettuce. Help yourself. Bread in the cupboard."

"Your mustard squirter's empty."

"I'll get some more. But I won't be home till four-thirty or so, okay?"

"Okay."

"Think you'll . . . still be there?"

"I don't know."

"All right. Well. I'll get some anyway."

"Some what?"

"Mustard. Listen, there's soup too. In the cupboard above the sink. And I think there's some macaroni and cheese in there. It's real easy, just read the box."

"Where's your remote?"

"My what?"

"For the TV."

"Oh, right. I don't have one. Sorry."

She didn't say anything.

"Well. Guess I . . . better get back to work. So . . . bye, Mary."

"Bye," she said.

I decided not to think, just work. And I did. I was all over those cars.

The TV was on.

I dumped the grocery bags on the kitchen table and walked into the living room, but she wasn't there. I headed down the little hallway, glanced in the bathroom, then went to the bedroom and stood in the doorway.

She was on the phone, laying across the bed facing away from me, wearing a towel around her head like a turban and one of my baseball undershirts.

She said, "I *told* you, I'll *see*, all right? God, quit—what? . . . I don't know. Prob'ly pretty soon. What time is it?"

I looked at my watch. "Twenty to five."

She whipped around. "Hi!" Then to the phone: "Well, Mom, I better go now. Nice talking to you, Mom. Bye." She hung up. "That was my mom."

"I could tell."

"Were you . . . standing there for a while?" She looked a little worried. She'd probably been telling her mom about this guy she met, this older guy. Or this *old* guy.

"Only for a second," I said.

"I just wanted to see how she's doing. She had this bad cold. I wanted to know if she got over it."

I told her that was really nice of her. I was beginning to see that under all the tough stuff Mary was a very sweet girl.

She rolled off the bed. "I borrowed your shirt, okay?"

"Looks good on you," I said.

"Yeah?" She held it out like a skirt and looked down at herself.

Such pretty little legs.

Then we both just kind of stood there.

"So. Did you eat?" I asked.

"Sandwich. You get mustard?"

"Yep. Lots of other stuff, too. Come on," I told her, and headed back towards the kitchen.

All kinds of shouting was coming out of the TV—a dozen people in a row of chairs, all mad as hell, pointing at each other and hollering and weeping.

"Aw, shut up," I told them, and slapped the Off button.

"This guy they had on before?" Mary said, heading for the stool by the counter top. "He says he's really a man—no, a *wo*man trapped in a man's body."

"Oh?" I started putting groceries away.

"But the thing is, the woman inside him is a lesbian."

"Huh."

"So he still goes for women. So, like, everybody thinks he's straight but he's really gay."

"Interesting."

"Can I have one of those?"

I was putting a six-pack of Old Style cans away. "You bet," I told her, and pulled two of them off the rings.

We snapped them open and I felt like saying something, like a little toast, something about *us*, nothing that would scare her, just *Here's to you and me*, something like that, but she was already putting hers away, a long drink with her head way back, then a belch and a satisfied sigh.

She kills me.

I took a drink and went back to my groceries.

"I was telling my mom about that picture you've got?" she said. "With you and that baseball player?"

"Nellie Fox."

"Right. I was telling her? And she thought that was, like, really special."

"She remembers Nellie Fox?"

"Oh, yeah. She said he was excellent. The most valuable player." She took another long drink.

I told Mary that was really good to hear, and it was, even though it pointed up that I was her mom's age. I said, "Because, you see, Nellie wasn't a flashy star, like a Mantle or a Mays. He was more of a throwback, if you know what I mean."

"Like you could just get rid of him?"

I laughed. "No, that's in fishing, Mary. A throwback in baseball is a guy who plays the way they used to play, back in the days of Ty Cobb and Honus Wagner and Willie Keeler.

See, back in *those* days—"

"Could I have another one?" she asked, holding out her empty beer can. "Sorry to interrupt."

She didn't believe in sipping them.

"Here you go."

"Thanks. My mom was saying how that picture's prob'ly worth something, him being such a big star throwback and all, you know?"

"She might be right," I said, putting away some cans of tuna. "There's this craze lately for baseball memorabilia—two thousand dollars for a rookie Mickey Mantle card, and such. And you know what I think that tells you? What that says?—"

"Rookie means first year, right?"

"Right. I think all this nostalgia you're seeing just goes to show—"

"Is that a rookie picture, that one you got?"

"Of Fox? No, that would be . . . let's see, I was seven, which was nineteen . . ."

"So it's prob'ly not worth that much."

"Money-wise? I don't know."

"Hundred maybe?"

"Possibly. It's the original picture, with his signature. So I don't know. 'Course, it'd be worth a lot more if he was in the Hall of Fame, which I'm sure he will be and it's just ridiculous that he's not there already. I mean, even if you look at just his numbers—but see, with Fox, that's only half the story, because here was a guy—how can I put this?—a guy who had the true, genuine spirit of the game. It just *shined* in him, you know? In everything he did out there, it just . . . I don't know, you had to see him, Mary. That's all I can say. There was just nobody else like him."

"What about Mickey Mantle?"

I laughed. What a cutie. "Well," I said, "he wasn't bad, either. In a different way, of course."

"You don't have any pictures of *him*, do you? He's, like, my favorite. Especially when he was a rookie. That's when I liked him the best."

I told Mary I was going to fix us something special: tuna-bacon-and cheese sandwiches, the bread lightly toasted, along with vegetable soup, apple sauce and V-8.

She stuck her finger down her throat.

I asked her what she would like.

"Spaghetti."

I told her I didn't have any spaghetti.

"Antonio's does."

So we went.

This being Friday, the place was pretty crowded, and I have to admit I felt a little funny in public with this young girl with a ring in her nose. A couple people yelled my name as we followed a waitress to a table in the back, but I didn't look.

Mary ordered her spaghetti and a Coke, and I chose a roast beef sandwich and a beer. While we waited I told her about my game tomorrow, against the Hounds From Hell, the team we're fighting for first place, with just a few games to go. She seemed kind of interested and even wanted to know what time the game started.

When her spaghetti arrived, here's how she ate. She kept her face very low over the plate, slurping up long splashy strands until her mouth was packed. Then she'd sit up straight and chew, swallow, slug some Coke, and down she'd go again. I was only about halfway through my sandwich when she let her fork drop onto her empty plate, wiped off her face with her napkin and sat back in her chair, looking exhausted.

I asked her how was it.

"Coulda been spicier."

Then Tony came over, in his white tux and phony accent.

"Stromboli! Ees-a nice-a to see you! And who's-a dees? You niece?"

"Tony, this is my friend Mary."

"You friend!" He gave a laugh, an Italian laugh. "Well, that's-a very nice. Ees-a nice-a to have a friend. And-a so young! Welcome-a to my restaurant," he told her.

"I already been here before," she said, still sitting back in her chair.

Tony cocked his head. "Ees-a that right? Funny I no remember, cuz-a we no get-a so many people with a ring in the shnozzola."

"You no like?" she said.

He gave another big laugh. "You Italiano too, eh? That's-a real cute." He turned to me. "So, how's the sandaweech, Stromboli?"

"Excellent," I told him. "Very tasty."

I was hoping he wouldn't ask Mary about her spaghetti, but he did.

She told him it was boring.

I said, "You can tell our waitress we're ready for our check now, Tony, okay?"

"Eet was-a *boring*?" he said to her.

She nodded, looking bored.

"What would-a you like eet to do?" he asked her. "Tell funny jokes?"

"It was blah," she said. "Like something out of a can."

He drew a long breath through his nose.

"Tony, our check," I said.

He leaned over the table. "*You*," he said to her. "*You* are like-a something out of a can—a *gar*bage-a can."

I said, "Hey," and got up from my chair. I couldn't let him talk to her like that. I said, "*Listen*," and then I just stood there pointing at him, trying to think what he should listen to.

Good old Tony, though. He stepped back from the table, holding up his hands, going, "Okay, take it-a easy, take it-a easy. I no wish-a to mess with *you*." He looked at Mary. "This guy knows-a *judo*."

Then he told us he'd have the waitress bring us our check right away, and hurried off.

I sat back down, shaking my head, trying to look pissed off and disgusted.

"You really know judo?" Mary asked.

"Enough to handle *him*," I told her.

She nodded at me—with a new appreciation, it seemed.

"Let's take this quiz," I said, wanting to leave the subject right where it was, and read her a question from my place mat: "What was the author Mark Twain's real name?"

She shrugged.

The answer was at the bottom. I gave her a little hint: "Samuel . . ."

"Scott Key," she said.

What a cutie.

Later on you should have seen me out on that dance floor at The Purple Angel. I'm not kidding, people were standing around *watching* me, checking out my moves—because I'll tell you something, I was cooking, and I mean with gas!

And afterwards back at the apartment? Well, I don't want to sound like Whitey Junior, so I won't even talk about it. Not a word.

It was about an hour before game time the next day and I was telling Mary about my ball glove, but I don't know how much she was listening. I was sitting on the ege of the bed in my Shopalot Sharks uniform, tightening up the finger laces on my twenty-five-year-old Wilson A2900 Nelson Fox model, just a wonderful little infielder's glove, and I was telling her about it while she stood in the doorway smoking a cigarette.

She'd been awful quiet since we got up, and kind of restless and distracted, smoking one cigarette after another.

"This glove is older than you, Mary," I told her.

"I'm gonna get a beer," she said. "You want one?"

"Not before a game. Thanks."

I went to the closet for my hat—which, if you saw it, you'd understand why I keep it there. It's white in front with foam reinforcing so it stands up nice and ridiculous, the logo a speeding grocery cart—for our sponsor, Shopalot Supermarket.

I was ready to go now and went out to the kitchen. Mary was standing at the window sipping a beer—actually sipping it. I told her we'd better be leaving.

She turned from the window. "I'm not gonna come, okay?"

It was kind of a blow. "Why not?" I said.

"I'm, like, just starting my period," she said. "And I get these real bad cramps? So . . ." She shrugged.

I dropped my glove on the table and went over to her. Women and their bleeding always gets to me, like they've been wounded. "I'm sorry, Mary. I didn't know." I took her in my arms. "You stay right here and take it easy."

She'd been acting so restless and faraway all morning and now I knew it was because she'd been worried about telling me she couldn't come to my game, not wanting to hurt me, even though *she* was the one bleeding and in pain.

"I'll be back," I said, holding her. "Okay?"

"How long?" she asked.

I held her tighter. She was really getting to me. "About two, maybe three hours," I told her. "Depends whether it's a high-scoring game, or if it goes into extra—"

"At least *two* hours, though, right?"

"Afraid so, sugar."

Sugar. It just came out.

Then we just stood there holding each other like I was going off to war.

"I'll be back, Mary," I promised again.

She looked up at me. "Bye, Hank."

I think it was the first time she ever called me by my name. It sounded wonderful. Then she gave me this kiss like she never did before—no tongue or anything, just real soft and sweet and sad—then gave me a little push and told me, "Go on."

I started walking off in kind of a daze.

"Here," she said, and tossed me my glove.

I caught it and just stood there by the door, looking at her.

"*Go*, will you?" she said.

I stepped outside on the landing, walked down the three flights of stairs and got in the car before remembering my keys. But I keep a spare car key in my wallet, so I used that, and drove away in a trance, wondering:

Can this be love?

5. I sat in the car for a while watching them take batting practice, feeling a little embarrassed returning after the way I'd left, after that pop-up . . .

"He's back and he's badder than ever!"

It was this black guy Walter, our left fielder.

"Hang on," I told him, and got out and grabbed my glove and spike shoes from the back seat. I wanted to walk in with somebody. That would be easier.

"How's your head?" he asked, and broke up laughing right in my face.

But you know? I laughed, too. It was *funny*, that's all, and I tried to think of something funny to say, but I'm not very witty so I just kept laughing, walking onto the field with Walter, staggering and laughing my ass off, probably overdoing it a little.

Our starting pitcher Redman was warming up beyond the first base dugout, throwing to our catcher Burlson.

I said, "Hey, you goddam redskin."

He just nodded and kept throwing, being in his "warrior mode," as he calls it.

Burlson goes, "How's the melon?"

I knocked on it. "Still there."

This was great.

I went into the dugout to change my shoes. Gordie was sitting there by himself, little wimpy-looking guy, making out the line-up. "Hey, Coach," I said. He likes when you call him that.

He looked up, said, "Lingerman," and looked down again.

"Play me or trade me," I told him.

He gave a big sigh. "I'm putting you down," he said, meaning down in the line-up, "but if Dunbar was coming you'd be sitting right fucking there," pointing to a spot along the bench.

I sat right fucking there and started putting on my spike shoes.

A beautiful day for a ballgame and I was in love.

I missed her already.

Spikes on, I stuffed a wad of chaw in my cheek, grabbed my glove and headed out there.

Burlson yelled, "Lingerman, lemme go take some swings," and tossed me the catcher's glove. So I finished warming up Redman.

Let me tell you about him. He's a great big long-armed guy in his mid-thirties, the oldest guy on the team after me, but Christ can he throw a baseball. Good control, too. Not much of a breaking ball, but he doesn't really need one here. I mentioned he was in his "warrior mode." What it is, he's got a little bit of Indian blood, probably about a drop, but he gets a lot of mileage out of it, especially during a game, going into this state of total Indian chief concentration, way inside, hardly speaking at all, except sometimes you'll hear him very quietly chanting to himself in Indian, going, "Hey-ah, hey-ah. Wey-ah, wey-ah." It's kind of funny because off the field he's an accountant, a CPA in fact, and he's got blonde hair and blue eyes. Some Indian.

"Let's see that hook," I told him, just to give my hand a break. He started throwing these sad little spinning dinkers. "Not a warrior pitch," I warned.

The two umps appeared on the field and told us to bring it in, and everyone headed for the dugouts.

Pretty good-sized crowd out there.

"Hey, Chicken Little! Hey, Chicklit!"

I didn't look.

"Chiiickliiit!"

I thought, *Tommy, you can't touch me today. I'm way too happy.*

Gordie read us the line-up: "Mitchell, shortstop! Lingerman, second base! . . ."

Love the sound of that.

Afterwards he reminded everyone that the team we were playing—the Haines Insurance Hounds From Hell—was tied with us for first place. "And as I'm sure you know," he added, "they're a bunch of fucking jag-offs who think they're hot shit. So let's go out there and kick their ass!"

And Brownie added, "Let's *do* it! Let's *do* it!" He's called Brownie because he's a brown-nose, but his name is Carl Brown so he thinks it's a *friendly* nickname.

We were home team today so we headed out to our positions.

I always get a certain feeling trotting out there at the start, you know? Kind of a sentimental feeling. Baseball is such a great old game.

Soon as we were set to go I started chattering to Redman, really more to help me than him. In fact, I've had pitchers ask me to shut up. Redman doesn't mind, though. The only thing he hears out there are the voices of his warrior ancestors, urging him on. He actually told me that once.

So I'm going, "All right, Redman, shoot 'em up, buddy, shoot 'em up, here we go, lotta hum, lotta pep, lotta fire . . ." And then the best thing that can happen at the start of a game to chase the butterflies—the ball was hit to me: a sharp grounder to my left and I scrambled over like a crab, scooped it up and fired to first.

It was good to be back.

Gordie was yelling and beating his hands together as we came in the dugout after the third out: "Let's go! Let's go! Let's kick their ass! Let's go!"

Sometimes I look at that kid to see if there's foam around his mouth. The thing he doesn't understand, you cannot play this game all clenched up. Fire in the belly, you bet, but you gotta stay loose, and somebody screaming at you all the time doesn't help you do that. But he's the one who got the sponsor—from his job as assistant produce manager at Shopalot—and he does all the phone-calling and money-collecting and takes care of the equipment and attends the league meetings and never plays unless we're shorthanded, so we let him scream at us.

"Let's jump on these jag-offs right away!" he told us, then trotted out to coach third base.

I grabbed a helmet and found my bat—which is easy to find, it's the only wooden one: a 33 inch, 34-ounce Louisvile Slugger, Nelson Fox model, same as the one I'm holding in that picture of me and Nellie. A bottle-bat it's called, very fat-handled, designed for punching out singles, and wood instead of metal because you've heard the expression, "the crack of the bat," right? Not the *ping* of the bat. And that's an important difference. I lose a few hits—the ball jumps better off the metal, no question. But *ping*, you know? I don't want any part of it.

I took some swings with a weighted bat in the on-deck circle, then knelt on one knee, leaning on my Louisville, and watched Mitchell pop out to the catcher.

"Next time," I told him as we passed.

"Yeah, yeah."

I stepped into the lefthanded batter's box, dug up a little trench for my back foot and made myself comfortable. I hold the bat about two inches up the handle, stand in a fairly deep crouch and do this rocking motion towards the mound while taking little half-swings—all Nellie Fox stuff. But like with the chewing tobacco, after so many years it's no longer imitation.

"Watch for the bunt!" the first baseman yelled, moving in closer, the third baseman creeping in too. They could tell I'm the type.

So I swung at the first pitch as hard as I could, missing it on purpose and letting out a loud grunt for added effect. That sent them back to normal depth. And as the pitcher delivered again, I thought, *Mary, this is for you*, and dragged a bunt up the first base line, right along the chalk, and all they could do was hope it trickled foul, which it didn't.

I must have been crazy to think about quitting this game.

There was still no score in the fifth inning when Redman made his first mistake, serving up one of his pitiful curve balls to this great big slob with his shirt hanging out, a guy they call Monster, who drove the ball out of sight.

And then you should have seen the asshole taking his sweet, up-in-your-face time around the bases. Three minutes it took him, no exaggeration. But that's an attitude you're seeing more and more, especially in the Bigs—which is just amazing to me. I mean, think back. Can you imagine, say, Al Kaline or Mickey Mantle or Henry Aaron behaving like that? Of course you can't.

Meanwhile, Redman was standing on the mound with his head bowed, arms at his sides, like a man in front of his child's grave. But what he's actually doing—which he told me once—he's observing his anger. That's how he put it: "I'm just observing my anger."

But by the time Monster finally made it around the bases, Redman wasn't observing his anger, he was observing Monster, watching him all the way into the dugout. So I'm yelling out, “Take it easy, Redman! Forget about him! We’ll get it back! No problem!”

But sure enough, he’s lost his warrior concentration and can’t find the plate, walking the next two batters. Then a wild pitch, advancing both runners, and here comes Gordie to the mound, our catcher Burlson joining them. I went over too, what the hell.

Gordie: “What’s the problem?”

Redman: “I got attached to my anger and it pulled me out of my center.”

Gordie: “So now what?”

Redman: “I have to get back.”

Gordie: “Back where?”

Burlson: “His center.”

Gordie sighed, and looked at me. “Lingerman, what’re you doing here?”

I shrugged.

“Let’s go, fellas!” from the ump.

Gordie told Redman, “Forget your fucking center. Just get the ball over the plate,” and trotted back to the dugout.

Well, he got the ball over all right, a big sweet lollipop that the batter drove into left center for a double, both runs scoring easily.

So that was it for Redman. Gordie sent him out to left field, trading places with Brannigan, who stopped the bleeding.

3–0.

And that was still the score as we headed in for the bottom of the ninth, Gordie shouting, "This is it! This is it! Do or fucking die!"

Brownie shouting, "So let's *do*! Let's *do*!"

Mancini led off with a bloop single to center. Then Brannigan hit a squibbler to the mound, the pitcher throwing to first.

So: one out, runner on second, we're trailing by three runs, and my hands and feet are getting moist because I might be batting.

Didn't used to be like that. I'd be sweating, sure, but from the juices pumping harder, that's all. Not this clammy kind of sweat.

Fitzgerald at the plate, Gordie yelling from the third base coach's box, "Come through! Come through!" But Fitz bats last for good reason and whiffed on three pitches.

Two outs now. Mitchell up, me on deck.

And while I'm kneeling there, leaning on my Louisville, I'm yelling all kinds of encouragement to Mitchell, but at the same time there's a sizeable part of myself hoping he makes the last out so it's not up to me.

Didn't used to be like that.

Mitchell worked the count to three and two.

"Good eye, Mitch!" I told him.

Ball four.

"Up to you now, Lingerman!" Gordie shouts. "It's aaalll up to you!"

I walked to the plate, feeling old and clammy.

But as I stepped into the batter's box, the catcher did me a big favor. "C'mon," he hollered to the mound, "let's get this geezer out of here!"

Amazing what a good clean shot of anger can do for you.

I jumped on the first pitch and drilled a single to right, scoring Mancini, Mitchell holding up at second.

3-1 now.

Redman the next batter. And from the way he goes striding up to the plate I can tell he's back in his warrior mode.

Sure enough, after fouling one off he rips a vicious, sinking line drive to left, and with two outs I'm off and running, the left fielder trying for a game-ending shoestring catch—but the ball skips under his glove and goes rolling out towards the fence, Mitchell scoring easily, and I round second base and come charging, head down, towards third, looking up as I approach, and there's Gordie in the coach's box windmilling his arm, screaming, "Go! Keep going!" and I do, rounding third and pounding for home with the tying run, and it looks like I'll make it, the way the catcher's just standing there.

Then my legs quit.

Ten feet from the plate my leg muscles turn into Silly Putty and I fall on my face. I try to get up but I can't. So I go crawling on my hands and knees, fast as I can, and I see the catcher slugging his glove, getting set for a throw coming in, and everyone's shouting, and I'm crawling and crawling, and just as I lunge for the plate the catcher takes the throw and swings his glove against my helmet.

"Out! He's out!" the ump hollers.

Game over.

I laid there.

"*Chiiickliiit!*"

I just want to be with Mary.

Driving home, that's all I keep thinking. Get back to Mary, back in her arms. Then I'll be all right. Then I'll be fine. I'll even tell her about the game—how it ended. Then tell her it doesn't matter. And tell her why: *Because I love you, Sugar.* And we'll hold each other. And she'll say my name. *Hank*, she'll say, *I love you too*. Then I'll be all right. Then I'll be fine.

The door was locked and I didn't have the key so I knocked and waited. Knocked and hollered her name. Then pounded. Then rammed with my shoulder. Rammed again. Stepped back to the railing, charged, rammed—and the door ripped open and I fell into the kitchen.

I got up and ran to the living room . . . ran to the bathroom . . . ran to the bedroom.

She was gone.

I stood there . . .

Then I noticed a paper plate on the wall, stuck on the nail where my Nellie Fox photo was supposed to be. There was writing on it.

Dear Hank,

Sorry about taking your tv and your picture. Guess I wasn't braught up very good. Oh well.

Anyway your a realy nice guy and I enjoyed meeting you and having sex with you.

Sincerely yours,

Mary

P.S. I hope you won your game!

Part Two

Karen

I was down on the floor doing lateral raises with Jane Fonda when Hank's boss called, looking for him. He said Hank didn't come in yesterday or today, didn't call, and there wasn't any answer when he phoned his apartment. "Any idea what's going on?"

I told him very coldly and politely, almost slipping into an English accent, "I'm afraid I can't help you, as Hank and I are no longer connected in any manner."

"Well, if you see him—"

"That's very unlikely."

"All right," he said and hung up, thinking, "Bitch," I'm sure.

I got back on the floor with Jane.

"*Get ready to speed it up! Here we go! Lift and down! Lift and down! C'mon, burn that fat! Work it! That's right! You're doing it!*"

I'd heard about Hank's little girl friend, from my cousin Phil the cop, so now I kept getting flashes of them *at* it, so hot and heavy he can't even answer the phone.

"*Don't stop! Keep going! Work those thighs! C'mon! Really get into it!*"

Or maybe something happened. Hank is an irresponsible child but not about his job, I'll give him that. So maybe something happened, something serious.

"Who cares!" I shouted.

"*That's it! That's the way! Hey, you're a winner!*"

But later on, folding clothes, I came to this baseball shirt he gave me for my birthday last year—an ugly thing, black and yellow with a bumble bee on the front, but I remember he said something sweet, something about me being his honey bee. I also remember how big on me it was and now I can barely button the damn thing—although I do think it shrank some.

Anyhow, I started worrying again and decided to try calling him. I figured if he answered I would just tell him George called, and get off. And if *she* answered, I'd ask if her daddy was home.

No one answered.

So now I'm standing there with this image of his phone ringing away beside the bed where he's lying with his eyes wide open and a little hole in the middle of his forehead, because Phil (who always has to tell me these things) said he'd seen this little bitch before, hanging out with some guy who works at the Purple Angel, a convicted dope dealer . . .

Well, I had to go to Shopalot anyway. Might as well swing by. It's on the way.

I rapped on Brian's locked door.

"Who is it?"

"That other person who lives here. I'm going to the store. I'll be back in a while."

"Get me a snow cone."

"I'm going to Shopalot. They don't have snow cones."

"Seven-Eleven does."

"But I'm not going there."

"Why *not*?"

I took a deep breath . . . and let it out. "Anyway, it'll melt," I said.

"Well get me *some*thing. A bag of Dorritos."

"How about *asking*, Brian, instead of—"

"Please get me a bag of Dorritos please."

"Much better."

"The *big* bag."

Hank has these eyes. I could never decide what color to call them. There's gray, and brown, and green, and some flecks of blue in there too. But such *sad* eyes. Soulful, I guess you could say—though not soulful like a saint or a poet, more like an old hound. Anyway, they're what got to me the first time I met him.

I had left my car at Whitey's Sunoco, needing an inspection sticker, and when I came back Hank walked up to me wiping his hands on a rag, telling me I had failed, that I needed a whole new exhaust system.

Jim had just left me about two months ago for one of his clients, Brian was wanting to join him, I'd begun this chocolate thing, and here was this sad-eyed man shaking his head, saying, "I'm sorry."

I burst into tears.

He brought me over to a bench in the corner and got me a glass of water, then told me in secret, "I know a place they'll do it for under a hundred and fifty. They're out on—"

"It's not the muffler!" I said.

"Well, not just the muffler, no. It's the whole exhaust system."

I went on crying. What a mess I was.

"Listen," he said, "if you want, I'll ask George to take a look, see what *he* thinks. But I doubt if—"

"I don't care about the muffler!" I bawled out.

"All the same," he said, "there's no way I can sticker you till you get the whole system replaced."

I couldn't stop crying.

"I mean, that's the *law*," he said.

I put my hands over my face.

Poor Hank.

"Listen, why don't I go get George," he said. "Let you talk to him. He's the owner. Okay?"

"I want to talk to *you*," I said through my tears, making room for him on the bench. Can you imagine?

Hank looked pretty bewildered but he sat down.

"Well," he said, "I can tell you this. The rest of the car's in tip-top condition. You'll probably need some new brake pads pretty soon and your tires are looking kind of worn, especially the right front one, but otherwise you're in great shape—except of course for the exhaust system. But hey, you know? Things could be worse. A lot worse. You could have cancer. Or be blind. Or . . . I don't know, paralyzed or something. You know?"

I nodded. I'd finally stopped crying. I found some Kleenex in my purse and wiped my eyes and blew my nose. Then I asked him, point blank, "Are you married?"

"Me? No. Was. For a short time. Years ago," he said.

I went straight ahead. "Would you like to have dinner with me tonight?"

It took him a moment to respond. Then he said, "Well, what's your name?"—as though that would determine his answer.

"Karen," I told him.

And I guess it was satisfactory, because he said, "Sure. Dinner. Sounds good. My name's Hank, by the way."

"I know," I said, nodding at his shirt pocket.

Then George yelled from somewhere, "Hank, finish that van out there. I got him started. He wants a fill. And check his oil."

We quickly decided: Antonio's, seven o'clock, meet in the bar.

He gave me back my car keys and told me the address of a muffler place out on Halsted.

That's how we met.

I pulled into the lot behind Hank's apartment. His car was there. I parked beside it, got out and dragged my fat butt up the three flights of stairs to his door . . . and found it open. Someone had broken in, violently. You could see where the wood in the frame was ripped. I started running down the stairs. But then I stopped . . . and went back.

I leaned my head in the doorway and called out, "Hank?"

No answer.

I stepped into the kitchen.

"Hank, you home?"

Silence.

I walked through the kitchen with scary-movie music in my head, like just before something horrible happens to the dumb chick who should have run straight to the police.

I entered the living room.

No one leaped out at me.

"Hank?"

Nothing, just the music in my head, growing wilder as I walked down the little hallway, glanced in the bathroom, then approached his open bedroom door . . .

And there he was.

He was sitting up in bed in his underwear with a photo album open in his lap. "Don't be mad," he said.

I don't swear very often but I swore. "Goddammit," I said, "didn't you hear me?"

"I'm sorry."

"Why the hell didn't you answer?"

"I should have. I'm sorry."

"Do you have any idea how frightened I was?"

"Of what?"

"I see your car and then I see the *door's* been broken open and then when I call—"

"I'm sorry."

"Stop *saying* that."

"All right."

"What happened? Why is the door like that?"

"I locked myself out."

"So you broke the door down?"

He shrugged.

"And what are you doing in bed?"

"Guess I just . . . didn't get up yet."

I told him it was four-thirty in the afternoon.

"That late?" he said. "Jeez, I better get up. Listen, thanks for dropping by. Sorry you got scared."

He wasn't getting rid of me that easy.

"George called, looking for you."

"Oh?"

"He said you didn't come in yesterday either."

"No, I've been kind of . . . taking it easy."

"Hank, what the hell's going on?" I asked, although I had a pretty good idea.

"Nothing much," he said, turning a page of his album.

"Where's your little friend?"

"Mary? Oh, she took off."

I stood there nodding my head, about ten different feelings running through me.

He tapped at a picture in his album. "This guy—he was our Little League manager. This is our team when I was, what, ten I guess, and I been trying to think of his name, but I can't think of it and it's driving me fucking crazy."

I could see that.

"Hank, listen to me," I said, although I wanted to just turn around and leave, let him have his little breakdown or whatever this was.

"Some kind of dago name," he went on. "Maroni . . . Mahoney—no, that's Irish. Macaroni?"

"Hank, *look* at me," I said, because I really and truly did have better things to be doing.

He looked up.

I asked him, "What're you going to do, just stay in bed the rest of your life because something bad happened to you?"

"I told you, I'm gonna get up. I just wanna finish looking at this."

I asked him if he'd eaten.

"I'm not hungry."

I thought maybe if I fixed him something, if I saw him eating, I'd be able to leave, hopefully for good. "What if I go out there and heat up some soup—will you eat it?"

He shook his head no, without looking up.

"Fine," I told him. "Fine. Stay there and rot. What the hell do I care?"

I turned around and headed back down the hallway.

"Karen?"

I stopped but didn't turn. "What."

"Don't be mad."

I drove to Shopalot and got bread, milk, fish sticks, frozen corn, a large bag of Dorritos, coffee, toilet paper, dish soap—and a gallon of chocolate chip ice cream, a box of fudge brownie mix, and a twelve-pack of Nestles Crunch Bars.

Hank

Marconi. That was his name.

I hung around with his son Mickey. That's Mickey next to me in the picture.

Mr. Marconi . . .

He called me over to the fence during Little League try-outs. Mickey was already on the team and Mr. Marconi was going to pick me. He already knew I could play. We all had a piece of paper with a number on it pinned to our backs, and all the coaches were standing along the fence with notepads. They each had a certain number of points and later at a meeting they would bid on us. Mr. Marconi called me over and started talking fast and quiet, saying I might as well not show too much out there, might as well not do too good. Save him some points. Get me cheap. "See what I'm saying, Hank?"

I said, "I guess."

"So don't catch everything. Drop a few. Drop a lot. See what I'm saying? And don't hit too good. Hit maybe one, but that's all. Okay? You wanna be on Mickey's team, right?"

"I guess."

"Attaboy. Go on now."

I wanted to go home.

But I did like he told me. He was over there watching.

But what I did, I'd make the catch, then give my glove a real deliberate-looking flip to drop the ball, then pick it up with a big phony head shake, trying to make it clear to everyone I was only pretending to be mad at myself, that I really meant to drop the ball, trying to make it clear that this was a hoax.

And at the plate I missed every pitch by a yard, by more than anyone could miss unless he meant to, and gave that phony head shake, and even said things like *Darn* and *Shoot* and *Jeepers*, as phony as I could, so people would want to know what's going on here, and I would tell them, I would say Mr. Marconi *made* me.

But nobody asked.

They probably just thought I was weird. Or that I really couldn't catch the ball or hit it.

When I went home I told my mom and she said that was a *terrible* thing for that man to do.

When my dad got home she told him, and I figured he'd give me all kinds of hell for going along with it. But all he said was Mr. Marconi better hold up *his* end now or he'd go have a talk with him.

And here's me from our high school paper, holding out my glove like I'm waiting for a throw. Underneath the picture it says: *Hank Lingerman, a sophomore who has broken into the varsity line-up, has made an auspicious start.*

I remember looking up “auspicious.” It meant “promising.”

Later, I kept hearing that word, “promising.”

Mr. Williamson, the Tigers scout, used it when he talked to me and my folks about signing with a Louisville single-A team. “The lad is very, very promising,” he told them. And my dad said, “How much you promising to pay the lad?”

And here, from a Jacksonville paper: I’m holding a bat and grinning, or squinting, or grimacing. Underneath, it says: *The Cranes have high hopes for second baseman Hank Lingerman, a promising young prospect recently acquired from the Red Sox farm.*

The Red Sox had called me that too.

I heard it for a long time, and then less and less, and then I didn’t hear it anymore at all, there being no such thing as a promising *old* prospect.

Here’s a picture I like a lot, from the Beeville paper. I’m turning a double play, runner sliding in, lots of dust: *Rustlers’ Joe Temple is out at second in an eighth inning double play, Lewis to Lingerman to Powley. The Bees won their third straight, 6–3.* I’m about thirty by that time, looking calm, good concentration, not promising anything, just playing ball.

Another action shot from Beeville: I’m laying down a bunt. Looks like a beauty . . .

I slept for a while, about an hour. Dreaming something.

I think I was dreaming about being here in bed.

Maybe I’m still dreaming.

Dreaming I woke up wondering if I'm still dreaming.
Wondering what's the difference.

Tony

I got this phone call at the restaurant just before we opened up for dinner. I was showing a new waitress around the place, kind of had my arm at her waist, a very sweet young girl named Patricia, very shy, very nice little titties.

Anyway, this phone call. I figured it's Helen, my all- knowing wife: *Get your hands off that child.* But it's this chick named Karen, used to be Stromboli Hank's numero uno, before this little punk bitch with the ring in her nose—except the ring's in *his* nose, right? Whatever. Anyway she wants to know would I go to Hank's apartment and talk to him. She says he won't get out of bed. I said maybe a doctor would be better to call, but she said he isn't sick. I said you mean except in the head. She said she didn't want to put it that way.

Or sick in the heart, more like it. I figured Little Miss Ring-in-the-Shnozz did him in. So I told her sure, no problem, I'll take a look at the patient. She said he probably won't answer the door but the lock's broke, so just walk in.

A very nice person, this Karen, giving a damn that way. And I'll tell you what. If she looked like she *used* to, about forty pounds ago, I'd go see what I could do about cheering *her* up, right? Whatever.

So I put my faggot nephew Brandon (a ring in the *ear*) in charge and drove over. But the closer I get, the more I'm wondering what the hell to say to a guy who won't get out of bed. So I dropped by this lowlife piss hole called Jerry and Larry's Sports Palace for a drink or two to loosen up.

"Momma mia, lookit this fuckin' meatball!" this guy Tommy says as I walk in.

I was wearing my tux from the restaurant, see, which kind of stands out in a place like this.

"Tommy, how you doing tonight?" I said, walking by. Which is is the way to deal with him. The guy is what you'd call a kind of human hocker.

I took a stool, skipping a space at the end of a row of the old gang, and ordered a martini, very dry, tossing down a twenty. "And give these gentlemen a beer."

"Thanks, Tony," etcetera.

"So," says Jerry, fixing my drink in front of me, "what the hell *you* doing here?" Jerry's identical to Larry, they're twins, except Larry minds his own fucking business.

I'm on a secret mission," I tell him. "A mission of mercy."

He gives a little snicker. "She's dying for it, huh?"

I have a certain reputation. Which I don't mind. Except it seems like everything I do gets back to Helen.

"It's not pussy," I tell him.

"So what is it?"

"None of your goddam business, all right? *Je*sus."

But instead of being insulted he gives a big laugh like he found me out: "So it *is* pussy!"

Now it's everybody's business.

"Got somethin' lined up?"

"Let's hear about it."

"That bitch with the blue fingernails, right?"

I said, "Look, this is a very private matter, okay?" And I told them about it.

I didn't go into why Stromboli won't get out of bed. But they did, telling me about this baseball game over the weekend where he tried to score or some shit and lost the game.

Which seemed like a pretty feeble reason for staying in bed, but then I never cared much for baseball.

"I *told* the guy to stop," this hyper little bird-faced kid named Gordie is telling me. "I got both my hands up, screaming at him—"

"Wait a second," this great big guy they call Redman says. "You were telling him to keep—"

"I thought somebody *shot* the sonofabitch," Tommy says, laughing. "The way he went down? I was looking around for a fucking sniper."

"And then he starts to *crawl*," Jerry tells me. "I was sitting near home plate and I could see his face. You talk about pitiful. That was the funniest damn thing I ever saw."

"No, listen," from this guy Randy Dunbar with the golden locks. "You want pitiful? Friday night. The Purple Angel. Lingerman. Out on the dance floor."

"Naw," says Jerry, and it *is* tough to picture.

"And you shoulda seen what he's with—some little bitch about my age with a ring in her nose."

"Right!" says Jerry. "I saw them at *his* place," pointing at me. "That's what he's prob'ly all in bed depressed about. She prob'ly dumped the fucker."

I ordered another martini and a fresh round of brews for the boys.

"Thanks, Tony," etcetera.

I told them whatever Lingerman's problem was, I'd have him back in action soon enough. And I meant it. See, I know how to motivate people, get them fired up with a purpose. I do it with my staff all the time. It's because I'm a very motivated type guy myself. I mean, let's face it, I own my own goddam restaurant, an establishment known all around the area and recently awarded four stars in the *South Suburban Times*, with a comment about "the debonair owner whose personal touch is evident everywhere."

I said, "In fact, you watch and see. He'll be back, right here"—I tapped the bar—"this very night." I sipped my drink.

"Bullshit."

It came from Tommy, at the other end of the row.

I remained calm. "You don't think so?"

"Nope," he says, and takes a drink of the beer I bought him.

I said, "Would you care to make a little wager, Tommy?" I knew I was stooping to his level but I couldn't help it. The guy just really gets to me. Always has.

He gave a shrug. "Sure. Why not?"

"How much, Tommy?"

"How much?"

"That's what I said, Tommy."

We're both leaning over the bar looking at each other past the row of guys, and they're looking back and forth, me to him.

Tommy says, "Twenty. Twenty dollars you can't get Lingerman in here tonight, on his feet and conscious—or anyway, on his feet."

Big laugh from the boys.

I said, "Make it twenty-five."

"Twenty-five it is."

"Shit," Gordie says. "I'm his *coach*. I'll bet *I* can get his ass in here."

"Is that right," I said.

"Yep," he says. Like that. "Yep."

I said, "Well, that complicates matters."

"Yep."

Little prick.

I came up with this. The three of us would put in twenty-five each. I'd go over there first. I'd have, say, half an hour with him—forty minutes to cover going and coming. If I can't get him up and over here in that time, then Gordie tries. And if he can't do it, Tommy wins.

Well, Gordie doesn't like it. Wants to know why I get to go first. "Let's flip for it," he says.

"Wait a minute," from Redman. He's been quiet through all this and I noticed him shaking his head a couple of times and now he's got something to say. It's about how wrong this is, what we're doing. "Laying bets on a man's soul" is the way he puts it. "That's gotta be wrong," he says. "That's gotta be pretty fucked up, you know?"

Gordie says, "You want in?"

So we ended up each giving Jerry twenty-five to hold, and to see who goes first he got out a pack of cards, shuffled them up, and dealt me a jack, Redman a nine, and Gordie a five.

"Two out of three," Gordie says. "Deal again. Here we go."

Jerry laughed and put the cards away.

"Story of my life," says Gordie. "Right there. You know? The whole fucking story."

"Well, gentlemen," I said, standing up, "my good friend Stromboli and I will be back very shortly."

Tommy goes, "Hold it a minute. Hold it."

"Too late to back out," I tell him.

"I know what you're gonna do," he says. "You're gonna go over there and explain about the bet and tell him you'll split the winnings if he comes back with you, right?"

I gotta be honest, it had occurred to me to do that, but only as a last resort. I said, "Tommy, Tommy," shaking my head with sadness, "give me a little credit, will you?"

"No." He told Jerry to put a can of Bud in a little bag along with a couple of Slim Jims. "And when I get back, I'm going with you," he told Redman. "And then with you," he told Gordie. "Where's your car?" he said to me.

Tommy doesn't drive. Never has. Never learned to. He's a security guard somewhere downtown and takes the train. But wouldn't you still want to know how to drive a car?

Anyway, I think this was the first time I'd ever been alone with him. It felt very unpleasant. I tried to make small talk.

"Looks like it might rain."

"Not a chance."

"I'm just saying it *looks* like it."

"And *I'm* just saying you're fulla shit."

Then when we got there we had a long pleasant climb together up Stromboli's stairs. He's on the third floor and Tommy had to stop every ten steps to cough his lungs out. The guy's only a few years older than me but holy Christ. Anyway, it gave me a good idea for my presentation: The Shortness of Life.

The door was busted open, like she said, and I walked right in, Tommy behind me.

"Hey, Stromboli!" I yelled, heading through the kitchen.

By the way, the reason I call him Stromboli, I think it means friend. And he is, since all the way back. He's the only guy I know that I can act like a bur*lone* around, the only one. That's another dago word, bur*lone*. Which I think means clown. I can be a bur*lone* around him because he's my stromboli, see? Now you can talk Italian.

Tommy behind me was yelling out, "Hey, Chicklit," which I don't know what *that* means.

We walked through the living room, then down this little hallway, a quick look in the shitter, then up to the bedroom.

I had to laugh, and I did.

Stromboli's laying there in his underwear—which is funny enough—doing the worst imitation of somebody sleeping I ever seen. Worse than my wife, even. He's got his eyes squeezed shut and he's snoring like in a cartoon—real loud, with a little whistle on the outbreath. And anyway did he really think we'd leave him alone because he's sleeping?

I walked over and shouted in his ear, "Stromboli!"

He opens his eyes, going, "Huh? What?"

Another Al Pacino.

Tommy by the door, looking at his watch, says, "Starting . . . right . . . now."

Stromboli looked a little scared. "Starting right now what?"

I sat on the edge of the bed. "Starting right now, my friend, you're gonna be a different man."

He scooted away a little. "What the hell's going on? What're you guys doing here?"

I took a softer approach: "Stromboli. I heard you were feeling kind of low. I came by to cheer you up. That's all. That's all I'm doing here."

He looked over at Tommy.

"He came for the ride," I said. "Never mind him."

Tommy gave this quiet little wheezy laugh. "Fuckin' Chicklit."

I said, "Tommy, keep your mouth shut please, okay?"

"Fuck you. I can talk if I want."

"No, you cannot," I told him.

Tommy put it to Stromboli. "All right if I talk in your house, Chicklit? Do I have your permission?"

Stromboli said it was all right.

Tommy thanked him. "And now," he said, "I think I'll have myself a Slim Jim. Would you care for a Slim Jim, Chicklit?"

Stromboli shook his head, no.

"They're very delicious," Tommy said, taking a bite. "And nutritious. Delicious and nutritious."

"Think of him as background noise," I said.

"Would *you* care for a Slim Jim, Tony?"

"The Shortness of Life," I said to Stromboli. "That's what I wanna tell you about, okay? The shortness . . . of . . . *life*."

"Twenty-one minutes," Tommy announced. "That's how short."

"Stromboli, look at me."

"Twenty-one minutes till what?" he asked.

Tommy laughed.

I kind of lost it at that point.

"Will ya fuckin' listen to me? I'm tryna tell you something here. Life—look at me, Stromboli—life is short, okay? I mean, just like *that*"—I snapped my fingers—"it's over. You're dead. You're a piece of rotting meat in the ground. And then it's too late, right? There was all this *life* you coulda been enjoying—and I don't mean just pussy. But now you're dead. You blew it. You spent all your time feeling sad and sorry over this, over that—"

"Twenty minutes," Tommy announced.

"Or else *mad* at people, you know? At all the assholes you're surrounded by. And not just mad when you're a*round* 'em but when you're *not* around 'em too, thinking how you're gonna show 'em up, how they're all gonna have to kiss your ass, and so you spend all your time putting something together to really show 'em, something really big. And when you finally put it together? Finally build your fucking tower? Finally *do* show 'em up? They despise you for it. 'Who the hell ya think you are?' they say. And you say, 'I'll *show* you who the hell I am,' and add some *more* fucking bricks to your tower. And you go *on* like that. On and on. And all this time you're getting older. And *mean*while—here's what I'm saying—meanwhile, what about just being *happy*, you know? Just plain old happy because, I don't know, the *sun* is out. Or fuck the sun, maybe it's raining out but you *like* the rain, the way it sounds, how it looks, puddles and such. There's nothing wrong with rain. Or even those goddam worms that come out all over the sidewalk afterwards. Nothing wrong with *any* fucking thing. It's all in your head. So why don't you get your ass out of bed right now and come and have a drink with me? I'm buying. What about it?"

Stromboli didn't answer right away. He just kept staring at me. Then he looked over at Tommy. Then back at me. Then he gave a sigh. "The thing is," he said, "I'm kinda tired, Tony. You know? Kinda sleepy. So I think I'll turn in a little early tonight. But thanks for the invitation. And thanks for dropping by. Both you guys. I appreciate it. Okay? Well . . . g'night."

And you know what he did? He laid back down, closed his eyes and, believe it or not, started up again with that bullshit snoring.

"Let's go," I said to Tommy. "Maybe he's got the right idea."

Tommy just kept chuckling and shaking his head, highly amused. And out in the kitchen he gave a holler: "Go, you fucking Cubbies!"

I dropped him off at the bar. Then I just drove around. I felt very agitated. I didn't feel like going back to the restaurant. I thought about getting drunk somewhere, but I didn't really feel like doing that either. I didn't even feel like getting laid. I knew where I *could* tonight, a *couple* places, in fact. But I just kept driving around.

It took a while but I was finally all right, or else just tired of driving. And I headed back to my four-star restaurant.

Hank

Maybe I should get up. Life being short, like Tony said.

Nice of him to drop by. In his tuxedo. His carnation was dangling but I didn't mention it.

What time is it?

Seven fifty-two.

I hate this angle of light. I should nail a blanket over the window. Karen was going to make curtains, for about a year.

She must have called Tony at the restaurant and told him I won't get up.

But maybe I should, life being short.

Funny seeing Tommy here. In his greasy old Cubs hat.

Go, you fucking Cubbies! he yelled.

Tommy and his Cubs.

Funny team for a nasty fart like him to love like he does, you know? With their baby-blue uniforms, cute little cub patch on the shoulder. In their pretty park, vines on the outfield wall, no lights for all those years—like they couldn't stay up late, being little cubbies.

I always had the flu or mumps or measles when I watched them, game time one-thirty. My mom would have me propped on the couch with pillows, wrapped in an afghan.

She'd watch too, sitting near.

I'd end up laying my head in her lap.

Watching the Cubs.

The Cubbies.

They were never in the running, so each game was just for itself, just for today. Just for us.

And the announcer Jack Brickhouse was perfect for the job, being a big sunny Cub-type guy himself, happy to be there: "in the friendly *con*fines of Wrigley Field."

And the P.A. man: this old white-haired guy named Pat Piper sitting in a folding chair against the wall behind home plate with his microphone:

Now batting . . . number fourteen . . . Ernie . . . Banks.

Ernie Banks. What a Cub-type guy *he* was: "Let's play two!"

Let's lose two!

Now and then my mom would feel my forehead with a long cool hand and ask me how I felt.

And I would tell her my throat is still sore when I swallow and I still have the chills—wanting to stay in the friendly confines, watching the Cubs lose, forever.

Redman

Tommy didn't like it but I drove to my house for some things I would need: drum, incense, eagle feather, and—to give Tommy a little part—gourd rattle.

Janet's Volvo was in the driveway.

"*Damn!*"

"Whatsa matter, Tonto?"

I pulled in as close as I could, concealing Tommy.

"Stay in the car. I'll be right back," I told him, and went in the side door.

She was standing in the kitchen in her bathrobe and slippers, holding a cup of tea in both hands.

She's a very small woman.

I'm a very large man.

But it never ends up that way.

"No classes tonight?" I said.

She said her cold had gotten worse, so after work she came straight home. "Where have *you* been?"

I told her a mix of fact and fiction, that I'd stayed late at the office and afterwards stopped off for a beer.

"At the Palace?" she asked, as I knew she would.

So now I simply lied. "No, this other bar."

Janet hates the Palace. "Tommy and them," as she puts it. For her birthday last month she asked for my word that I would never set foot in there again. She said that would be the most wonderful gift I could possibly give her. And what could I say? It was her thirtieth.

"What other bar?" she asked me now.

"I forget the name," I said. "It's near the office. Nice place. You'd like it. Lotta ferns." I headed downstairs where I keep my things. "I have to go back out for a while," I shouted up. "Just for about an hour."

She came down, wanting to know where.

"Hank Lingerman's."

Wanting to know why.

I told her. I said, "Because he's feeling very depressed, very . . . de*feated*," neglecting of course to mention the bet, but that wasn't really part of it anyway. I picked up my box of ceremony items. "I'd like to see if I can help him."

"By doing your medicine man routine?"

"Yes," I said, feeling my face turning red.

"My God, he's serious."

I hate when she does that, refers to me as "he," while I'm standing there in front of her.

I told her I'd see her in a while and headed past her for the stairs, wanting to get out before she could weaken me further.

But she was right on my heels. "And he *wants* you to do this for him? This—this—"

"Healing ceremony. My first client." I was at the door. "Wish me luck."

Then goddam Tommy honked the horn.

"Who's that?" she said.

"Out there? That's . . . Hank. Listen, I'll see you in about—"

"Hey, Tonto!" Tommy hollered. "Let's go!"

She looked at me with a smirk of utter disgust. "That's Tommy," she said quietly. "Isn't it."

"I'll be back in an hour."

She slammed the door behind me.

"Little Caesar giving you a hard time?" Tommy asked as we drove away.

I told him I didn't want to talk about it.

She makes me feel foolish, weak, and small, then angry at how foolish, weak and small she makes me feel. And as I drove along I tried to *observe* my anger, as Troublemaker is always telling us to do. Anger disempowers, he says, because it draws us away from our center, but a warrior learns to observe his anger and thereby keep his distance from it, remaining in his center, where his true power lies.

So that's what I was trying to do.

Troublemaker, by the way, is the workshop name of our Men's Group leader, Dr. Carl Shapiro, author of *Cry of the Wolverine: On Awakening the Ancient Warrior Within*. We meet every Sunday evening, sitting on the floor with our drums in a large bare room at a Holiday Inn downtown. Dr. Shapiro named himself Troublemaker because he upsets people, disturbs and stirs them up—because we *need* to be, or we'd stay asleep our entire lives.

We *all* gave ourselves names the very first session, after

sitting in the dark in silence for twenty minutes, searching within. The name I found down there was Throws Smoke. It describes my warrior nature when I'm out on the pitcher's mound for our town team, the Shopalot Sharks.

Among my teammates I'm known simply as Redman.

Tommy calls me Tonto.

Janet calls me Bob.

I should mention that I *am* an actual Indian, a Lakota Sioux. Not a full-blood, however. I've worked it out and it comes to one-sixteenth. But the Sioux were—and still are—a great, noble race, and even a drop of their blood contains much *wochangi*, or spiritual power.

I was feeling better, having observed my anger, and began to sing: "Hey-ah, hey-ah! Wey-ah, wey-ah! Hey-ah—"

"Save it, Tonto, will ya? Jesus."

He was right. Save it. I kept quiet, letting it grow.

Hank was curled up asleep in his underwear, snoring loudly.

Tommy told me to go tickle his feet with my feather.

I looked at him.

"Let *me*, then."

But Hank suddenly sat up.

"Chicklit! Hey. Brought you another visitor," Tommy told him.

"How you doing, Hank?" I said. "How you feeling?"

He nodded, looking very gaunt, gray-faced and dull-eyed, needing a shave, his hair every which way, his spirit in serious decline.

"We'll only be here half an hour," Tommy promised him. "Right, Tonto? Starting now, which is eight twenty-five."

I set my box on the floor by his bed. I had decided to perform the warrior ritual I do in the basement at home before each of my ball games. "Hank, I'm going to light some fragrance," I said, and set a little cone of sandalwood incense in a bowl and held a match to it. Sage would be more appropriate, I know, but it's hard to find. "This is to purify the area," I explained.

"*That's* a good idea," Tommy remarked, by the door.

Kneeling in front of the bowl I waved my feather in the smoke to spread it around, calling out, "I burn this in praise! A sacred praise I am making!"

Hank said quietly, "Redman?"

"Please don't interrupt," I told him, and continued: "In praise of Wakan Tanka! Who dwells at the center of the universe! Who dwells at the center of our hearts! Who is *not* a subject for laughter!"

I added that last line for Tommy.

Now for the drum.

I removed it carefully from the box, such a beautiful thing, gray feathers hanging all around the rim. I bought it at our first workshop, from Troublemaker; he was selling them along with his book.

I told Hank he was going to have to join me on the floor now.

He started putting up a fuss, saying he appreciated what I was trying to do, whatever it was, but that he had an awful headache, and so on.

I said, "Hank, listen to me. It's not enough to just sit there and watch. This isn't some sideshow for the tourists. This is the real deal. So I want you to come down here on the floor right now. Let's go. Come on. Right now."

He did some more complaining but he finally got down on the other side of the drum, and I handed him a stick.

"And Tommy?" I said. "This is called a gourd rattle. You can stay over there but I want you to help us out while we drum. Like this," giving the gourd a few rhythmic shakes.

"You're out of your fucking mind," he said.

"Here," I told him, "catch."

He caught it.

"Okay," I said. "Now. Hank? I'll establish the pace. Then you jump right in and bang away. I'll also be singing, and I want you to feel free to join me in that as well. Tommy, hold off on the rattling till we start, okay? Thank you. All right, let me just tell the Father Spirit what we're up to here."

I spread my arms, closed my eyes, raised my face toward the Land of Elders, and loudly called out a little piece I wrote myself:

"Grandfather! We are going to drum and sing for you! We are going to drum and sing with all our hearts! We are going to wake up the spirit that is sleeping inside us! The spirit you have given us! The flying spirit of the eagle! And the roaring spirit of the bear! And the cunning spirit of the fox! Which together make the spirit of the man! Of the warrior! Grandfather, help us to wake this spirit! To make this spirit live in us again!"

Then, keeping my eyes closed, I struck the drum, hard, and began a strong and steady rhythm, like the beating of a warrior's heart, crying out loud and high:

"Hey-ah, hey-ah! Wey-ah, wey-ah! Hey-ah, hey-ah! Wey-ah, wey-ah . . . !"

And soon it began to work, as it almost always does: the heart like an egg begins to slowly break open, then out crawls a new man, a warrior, who stretches and fills up the chest and the head and the arms and the legs of that hollow man.

"Hey-ah, hey-ah! Wey-ah—"

Someone poked me in the shoulder.

It was Hank, standing over me, holding the phone.

"Your wife," he said.

She told me to pick up some Tylenol and orange juice on my way home, but I knew why she was calling: to see if I was really there and not at the Palace.

"How's the pow-wow going? Doing the trick?" she asked.

"It was," I said.

"Before I interrupted. Sorry, Chief. Carry on. Orange juice and Tylenol." She hung up.

Hank was sitting on the edge of the bed with his drum stick, Tommy leaning in the doorway with his gourd rattle, both of them looking at me.

I spoke in the phone: "Is that right? Well, let me tell *you* something, little lady. I don't appreciate being checked up on. I mean, who the *hell* do you think you *are*? . . . That's right: my wife. Good answer. So let me explain something, Wife. If you want to *keep* that job, I suggest you stay the hell off my goddam *back*. And I'll tell you something else. The three of us—me and Hank and, yes, your good friend Tommy—you know where *we're* going after this? The Palace. That's right, the Palace. So I can't really tell you *when* I'll be home tonight, honey—if at all!" And I hung up.

Tommy loved it. "Ton*to*! Layin' down the *law*! On the fuckin' *squaw*!"

I dumped my drum back in the box, feeling too fraudulent now to continue with the ceremony, just wanting to go get drunk.

"You coming?" I asked Hank, taking the stick out of his hand.

"Well, no, I don't really—"

"Leave him be," Tommy said. "We've bothered the poor fuck enough, for Chrissake. You take it easy, Chicklit. I'll drop by a little later, see how you're doing."

"That's all right," Hank said. "I'm fine. Really. Don't bother."

"Hey, it's no bother, Chicklit, believe me," Tommy assured him.

I told Hank I was sorry this didn't work out.

He shrugged.

Then we left, Tommy ahead of me doing a rumba all the way to the stairs, shaking the gourd rattle, chanting "Go-you-fuckin-Cub*bies*. Go-you-fuckin-Cub*bies* . . ."

Hank

Redman forgot his bowl of incense.

He said it was to purify the area, and Tommy said that was a good idea.

So I'm starting to stink.

It would stink a lot worse if they came and found me dead.

Which is probably all they'd say: "Jesus, stinks in here!"

Maybe someone would say, "Poor old fuckin' Hank." And somebody else say, "Yeah."

Karen might cry a little. Or maybe a lot. I don't know. Hard to say.

Mary wouldn't cry. Are you kidding?

I guess my dad would cry. His only child.

The stone would say:

Hank Lingerman
1951-1991

And that's all. What else *could* it say?

I called my dad.

"Hello, who's this?"

"Hey, Whitey."

"*Well.*"

"How ya doing?"

"Just fine, Hank."

"How's the weather?"

"Got up to one hundred and three degrees out there today."

"Wow."

"But see, it's dry heat, so that's all right. What about you?"

"Rain."

"Ah, well."

"Listen, Dad . . ."

"Yeah?"

"I was wondering . . ."

"I'm listening."

"How's Carlotta?"

"You were wondering how's Carlotta?"

"How's she doing?"

"Well, she's . . . doing fine, Hank. I'll tell her you were asking."

"Good. And the other thing is . . ."

"We went down to the pool for a while today."

"Oh?"

"You oughta see her in her bathing suit. Oh, brother!"

"Ha."

"And you should see the *looks* we get from those geezers down there."

"Huh."

"I always wanna say to 'em, 'That's right, she *ain't* my daughter.'"

"Right. Listen . . ."

"Tell it straight to their faces."

"The other thing I wanted to ask you about, Dad, besides Carlotta . . ."

"Yeah?"

"It's about this guy I know. I don't think you ever met him. He's about my age. Name's Charlie? Charlie . . . Chicklit."

"Charlie Chicklit?"

"Right."

"So what's his problem? Besides his name."

"Well, it's a little hard to describe. I mean it's kind of strange, his . . . behavior."

"What is he, queer?"

"No, he's not queer, Dad."

"Well, what's he doing? Giving you trouble?"

"No. It's just . . . it's like . . . I don't know, he just doesn't wanna get out of *bed*. Like he doesn't see any real good *reason* to."

"To get out of bed?"

"Right."

"How the hell do *you* know?"

"Know what."

"About this guy and his bed. What is he, your *boy*friend or something? Is that what you're trying to tell me here?"

"Dad . . ."

"Jesus Christ, Hank, I don't think I can handle this. I really don't think I can. I'm sorry. You're my one and only and all that, and I know maybe I haven't always—"

"Dad, listen to me. *Please*?"

"I'm listening, Hank. Don't shout at me. This is painful enough."

"Dad, I'm not queer. And Charlie's not queer either. He's just . . . I don't know . . . going through something. And the way I know about it is because some of us from the bar have gone over there to try and cheer him up a little, or at least get him out of bed. But he just says, 'Thanks for dropping by.'"

"And he's not queer?"

"No. Honest."

"And you're okay too?"

"Yes."

"You scared me, Hank."

"Sorry."

"I don't know what I would do."

"Well, you don't have to worry about it."

"Can I give you some advice, though?"

"Actually, I was hoping you could advise me about Charlie."

"This *is* about Charlie. Stay away from him. He sounds like a nutcase."

"He's not a nutcase, Dad."

"No?"

"I don't *think* he is, anyway."

"So how long's he been like this? In bed like this?"

"Since Saturday. So that makes it . . . What's today, Wednesday?"

"Tuesday. Maybe the guy's just lazy. Ever think of that?"

"He's not lazy. I know him and he's not."

"Then I don't know what to tell you, Hank."

"Okay. Well . . ."

"How are *you* doing?"

"Me? I'm fine. Real good. Listen, I better get off now. Believe it or not, I think I left my car window open again."

"Jesus, Hank. What the hell's the matter with you?"

"I don't *know*, okay? I don't *know*!"

"Don't shout at me, boy. I told you about that."

"I'm sorry. I just . . . I'm sorry."

"Something wrong, Hank? Something you're not telling me about?"

"No, I'm fine. I'm just . . . I guess I'm just a little worried about Charlie, that's all."

"Well, I'm sure he'll be all right."

"Think so?"

"I'm sure of it. Meanwhile, let me give you some advice. You listening?"

"Yes. I am."

"When you get out of the car, I don't care whether there's a cloud in the sky or not, roll your window up. Just roll the sonofabitch up. Get in the habit so you don't even have to think about it. All right?"

"All right."

"Attaboy."

"Bye, Dad."

"So long, Hank."

Gordie

This sucks.

Everyone's gone and I'm sitting here watching World Federation Wrestling with Jerry.

"A lotta that shit is fake," he says.

Then Tommy and Redman finally get back, with no Lingerman, which is excellent and I'm ready to go, ready to win this thing. I already thought about what I'm gonna say to him: all about Life being like a baseball game. I got everything covered, even bunts and shit.

But fucking Redman, he slams his big hands on the bar and hollers, "*Beers all around*"—like the place was packed instead of just Tommy, me and himself. So of course, Tommy wants to stay for that, and for another free round after that. Which was like a real lotta fun, Redman tossing down shots with his beer and getting into his favorite subject, how we fucked over the Indians.

"Oh, my people," he goes.

When we finally get there, Lingerman's curled up under the bedsheet, head and all.

"Visiting hours are over," he says.

"Got a special visitor for ya, Chicklit," Tommy tells him. "Do you recognize . . . *this* voice?" and he puts his hand on my shoulder.

I felt goofy. I said, "It's me. Gordie. Hi."

"Could you turn off the light please?" he asked.

But Tommy just went on, "Gordie wants to talk to you, Chicklit. He promises he'll only be half an hour. So go ahead, Gordie. Tell Chicklit what you wanted to say," and gives me a little push, like I'm a kid in front of Santa Claus.

I went over by Lingerman's head under the sheet and said, "Hank, y'know, Life is like a baseball game, isn't it? When you think about it? I mean, first of all, you got your . . . got your . . ."

I forgot how it started. With pitching? No, it was the *manager*—that was it. But how'd it go? I couldn't fucking remember. Shit, it was a great speech. But with Tommy standing over there I felt like I had stage fright. So I skipped all the way to the ending, which I knew really good:

"So anyway, listen. Why don't you come out of the dugout, old buddy, and get back on the field, back in the Ballgame of Life! Maybe you'll whiff or maybe you'll ding one, but either way it's better than sitting on the bench. So come on, slugger, it's *your* turn at bat. Step up to the plate. Get up there. Come on. Get up. Get up, man!"

And he did.

Not all the way, but he threw off the sheet and swung his legs over and sat on the edge of the bed, looking all bony and old in his underwear, and practically gagging me with the smell he sent out.

But I'm like, "Attaboy, attaboy. Now get dressed. Come on. We'll go have a beer. C'mon, old-timer, you can do it. I know you can."

He held up his hand for me to be quiet.

Then, looking down at the floor, he said in this tired voice, "All you guys . . . coming over like this . . . there's something going on." He looked at me. "Tell me what it is."

I told him, "Hank, I don't know about these other guys, but all I want, like I said, is to see you back in the ballgame. And you know that's the truth, buddy."

Tommy sniffled like he was crying.

"And hey," I said, "speaking of ballgames," and told Lingerman how tomorrow night's game is a big one, how we're only a game out of first place and we really need this one. "But we can't do it without ya, buddy," I said, even though I was definitely putting Dunbar at second base whether Lingerman showed up or not. Go with youth, you know? Somebody who can at least make it all the way around the bases.

He jerked his thumb towards Tommy. "Why's *he* always along?"

Now the shit got *really* thick. I said, "He don't wanna say it, Hank, but you know what? He's kind of concerned. Kind of worried about you. And that's the truth. He just don't wanna say it."

He slid his eyes towards Tommy.

Tommy blew him a kiss.

Lingerman gave a big tired sigh and laid back down.

"Don't, man!" I told him.

He pulled the sheet up over himself again.

"Aw, shit. Come on," I said. "You were doing good. You were getting up, getting back in the *game*. Come on. Get up, will ya? Don't do this to me."

"Go away," he said.

I had another card.

I told him, "All right, go ahead. Stay in bed. Hide your face. *Be* a quitter. Only don't expect to be in *my* fucking line-up, because I don't want quitters on *my* club. So if you don't wanna be sitting the bench, buddy, you better get your ass out of bed, and I mean now."

I waited.

"Right . . . fucking . . . now," I said.

And waited.

Then I just let loose on him, what the hell. I called him a loser. I called him an old, old man. I told him how hard we were all laughing tonight in the bar, laughing at *him*, at how pitiful he was, crawling on the ground like a —

"Shut up, you."

From Tommy.

I looked at him. "Whaddaya mean?"

"Let's go," he said. "You're through here. Come on."

"Bullshit." I looked at my watch. "I got another . . . thirteen minutes."

He shook his head. "Game over. Bedtime. Come on." And walked off.

"No *way*, man," I said.

Lingerman poked his head out. "What're you talking about? What's going on?"

I told him none of his fucking business and ran after Tommy. I said, "Hey, if you're quitting, I win."

He kept walking.

"No other way," I said.

He stopped at Lingerman's fridge and grabbed a beer and stepped out on the landing with it. I didn't know what he was up to, but I kept on making my point: He quit. I won.

He set his beer on the railing, lit a cigarette and looked off like I wasn't there.

But I stayed right on him: "No other way, man. No other possible way. You quit. I won. No other way."

He blew out some smoke. "Then get outa here, ya fuckin' maggot."

I took the stairs two at a time, got in my car and drove like a bat to the Palace, because with Jerry you never know when he's closing, especially if nobody's there and nothing's on TV.

So of course I caught a fucking freight.

It was one of those kind that creep along, creaking and groaning, and then starts going even slower, and slower, and then just stops. And sits there for a while. And then starts crawling the *other* fucking way.

I laid my forehead against the steering wheel, wondering, *Why me, Lord?*

Anyway, I made it. He was still open. Redman was still there—plastered, sitting by himself in a booth doing his Hey-ah, wey-ah. When he saw me he started yelling for me to come over but I told him hang on and went up to the bar and told Jerry I won, so give me the money.

"So where's Lingerman?"

I explained about Tommy quitting.

He didn't buy it. "Why would he quit?"

I told him I had no idea. Which I don't. I mean, he couldn't wait another thirteen minutes? I don't understand.

Jerry said he'd have to check my story with Tommy tomorrow.

I told him, "Never mind Tommy, check it out with Lingerman. *He'll* tell you. Call him up right now."

He said no, he might be in bed.

I said, "Of *course* he's in bed."

He wouldn't call, though.

I gave up and told him to give me a beer. I guess I could wait a day, what the hell.

Meanwhile Redman keeps yelling at me to come over to his booth. "Wanna tell you something," he goes.

I said, "Not if it's about Indians." I'm sick of his fucking Indians.

"C'mere, man," he said.

I went over. I gotta humor the guy. He's done a great job for me on the mound this year and I want it to continue. We're only a game out of first, with four games to go.

I sat down and he says to me, "And what is Life *now*? What is it *now*?"

I said, "It's like a baseball game. First of all, you got your—"

"There is no longer any *center*," he went on. "The sacred tree is dead!"

"Yeah, well."

"Know who said that? Know who said those words?"

"Some Indian?"

"Black Elk. A medicine man of the Oglala Sioux. A man of great—"

"I'm outa here."

"Wait. Don't go. C'mon."

I told Jerry I'd be back for my winnings tomorrow, and drove home.

I really wanted that money tonight, though. I didn't *need* it tonight—I was only going home. But I just wanted to hold it, you know? Hold it in my hands and know that I won, that tonight I was a winner. They lost and I won. Then I could go to bed thinking maybe everything's *not* against me. And could sleep.

Hank

Tommy came walking back slow and stood in the doorway.

"Drive me home."

He lives four blocks away.

"Can't you walk?" I said.

He shook his head, no.

I told him I was awful tired. "How about calling a cab?"

Thing is, if I stepped outside, everything would be set in motion again. And I wasn't ready yet. I needed more time. To sort things out, you know? Another day or two. Then I'd go out there. Two or three more days, that's all.

I told Tommy I'd pay for the cab, if that was the problem.

He shook his head. "Let's go."

"I'm sorry, but I can't," I said. "Please turn the light off when you leave." Then I rolled onto my stomach, gathered the pillow in my arms, and tried to send myself to sleep: ninety-nine, ninety-eight, ninety-seven . . . but I could feel him still standing there, waiting. And when I snuck a look he winked at me.

"Sonafabitch!" I yelled, and got up.

I grabbed my ball pants from the pile on the floor and yanked them on, then followed him barefooted down the hallway, through the living room, through the kitchen . . .

"You oughta get this door fixed, Chicklit."

I agreed.

Tommy

Chrissake he'd a stayed in bed til he fucking starved to death. The guy takes everything way too serious. Always has. In the car I told him about the bet and gave him half a Slim Jim. "Eat this. It's delicious and nutritious." And he did, he ate it right up. So I gave him the other half, what the hell.

After I got out I told him, "Just remember one thing, Chicklit."

"What." He looked interested as hell.

I said, "Go . . . you fucking . . . Cubbies."

He sighed and drove away.

I laughed all the way into the house.

Fucking Chicklit.

Anyway, he'll be back at work tomorrow, watch and see. And I'll bet he never even thanks me.

I fed Santo the cat and went to bed.

But I couldn't sleep. Sometimes you're *too* tired, you know? So I laid there thinking about Vanna.

She calls me Tom-tom . . . tells me I'm the one . . . the only one . . .

Afterwards I had a cigarette.

But then I still couldn't sleep. So I started thinking about the Cubs, what they need.

A bullpen.

A shortstop.

Speed on the bases.

Belief.

The last time the Cubs won the pennant was nineteen forty-five, the year before I was born, and I've taken an awful lot of shit from people about that. But I just smile and say Fuck you, and I'll tell you why. Because deep in my heart I know that someday, before I die, the Cubs will rise again. They'll win their division, win the playoffs, and be National League Champions. Then in the Series they'll kick the living fucking Jesus out of the American League team, hopefully the White Sox, and be *World* Champions.

It's gonna happen. I know it is. And I don't mind waiting. In fact, I'll tell you a secret. I hope it don't happen for a while yet.

Because *then* what?

Know what I mean?

Part Three

Hank

1. "Where the hell you been?"

Soon as George said that, I knew I still had my job.

I told him, "Sorry."

"See what I was just gonna put in the window?" He held up a *Help Wanted* sign. "You couldn't even call?"

What could I say? For one thing, I've always had this feeling George thinks I'm a little strange, and I didn't want to add to it.

But I think I did.

I told him I'd been in a coma since Saturday.

"A coma," he said.

"Got hit by a pitch," I explained.

"Another one?"

"Right."

"And you went into a coma?"

"Just . . . kind of a minor one."

He blew out some air. "Yeah, well, I guess even them minor ones can be a bitch." Pretending to believe me.

"Tell me about it," I said, pretending to believe he believed me.

We had our coffee and talked about work, how far behind we were, thanks to me and my coma. Then I followed him into the car bay, where he showed me a tricky little problem with the ignition on an '89 Skylark . . .

Around noon it started raining and kept up hard all day. It was supposed to continue through tonight, meaning no ballgame, and I have to admit I was glad. My ass was dragging.

I would have gone, though. I wasn't quitting. I'd made up my mind: balls falling on my head or my legs collapsing under me, I didn't care, I was gonna finish the season. We were one game behind the first-place Hounds, just a few games to go, and I wanted to contribute. I still felt like I could.

At home I showered and put on my bathrobe, made some soup and set it on the coffee table in the living room—cozy, with the rain still coming down. And then I actually took a step towards the TV, where it used to be . . .

First Mary stole my heart and then she stole my TV and my Nellie Fox photo. She made believe she liked me, that I appealed to her, but how could I appeal to her? It was just so she could steal my stuff. I pictured her sitting right now on a couch somewhere, naked with some naked stud—who probably helped carry the TV—watching soap operas, laughing every time she thinks about this old man she made such a fool of, how she had him calling her *Sugar* . . .

I flipped the coffee table over, soup and all, then looked around for things to throw, things to break, but there wasn't much, just the little table lamp. I stomped over and picked it up and yanked out the cord—but then I didn't feel like throwing it. Which pissed me off and I gave it a heave.

I stood there for a minute breathing hard.

Then I went and picked up the lamp. I put it back on the little table and plugged it in again. Not even the fucking bulb broke.

I went and got a sponge for the soup.

I decided maybe it's a good thing, no TV. I would read. Improve the mind, you know? Never too late. I'd go to the library tomorrow and see what they had for books. Meanwhile, though, there wasn't anything to read in the whole apartment, not even a *TV Guide*.

But then I remembered I did have one magazine, up in the closet, in a plastic sleeve.

Sport, April, 1958, Nellie Fox on the cover: big smiling bright-eyed face, Sox cap tilted back, plug of chaw bulging his cheek. With an article inside: "Little Nellie's a Man Now," including photos and stats. I hadn't looked at this in years. There's a picture of him at sixteen in his town team uniform, and a picture with Lucky Evertt, his bowling alley partner, and a good shot of him turning a double play. But the one that really struck me was the picture with his wife and kids.

Nellie's down on all fours on the living room carpet with his baby daughter riding on his back, his older daughter and his wife Joanne holding the little girl steady, and everyone's smiling.

A family.

A happy family.

I put my head in place of Nellie's, and Karen's in place of Joanne's, and on my back a little Henrietta, Brian helping hold her steady.

I tried to get all of us smiling.

The librarian the next day looked at me funny when I put the book on the counter. I was straight from work so I thought maybe I smelled bad.

"Do you wish to borrow that?" she asked.

She was a very small old lady, really tiny.

I said, "Yeah. Is that okay? I'll bring it back."

The book was *Webster's New World Encyclopedia, Pocket Edition*, although you'd need one hell of a pocket. Nine hundred and thirteen pages it had. I figured I'd read the whole damn thing, all the way through, A to Z. It would take a while, especially the way I read. But when I finished? Ask me anything you want, from Apples to Zippers.

But she told me I couldn't take it out because it was a reference book. She said if there was something in particular I wanted from it, they had a copy machine, ten cents per.

I told her I wanted to read the whole thing.

I think she was impressed. "That would be quite a formidable task," she said.

I told her that was the point, to form the mind. And since there wasn't anyone else around, I went ahead and told her about my TV being stolen.

"Burglars?"

"Sort of an inside job."

"Oh?"

For a moment I actually felt like telling her the whole sad story—about Mary, and my "coma," and especially about finally knowing what I really wanted now: a family. A good solid happy family, like Nellie's. I'd like to hear what she thought about that. She seemed pretty intelligent.

But I just met the woman, so all I said was, "I guess I'll go take a table."

"Why don't I show you our reading room?" She lifted up a section of the counter and came through, although she could have just stooped a little and walked under it, she was so small.

I followed her with my book all the way to the back, through an open doorway, into this room with a shiny hardwood floor and throw rugs and a grandfather clock and sofa chairs and paintings on the walls.

"Here we are."

You could tell she was proud of it.

"Very . . . *nice*," I said, with my puny vocabulary. But maybe this book would help.

"Whoever stole your television, I wish he would steal everyone else's as well," she said, looking around sadly.

And it *was* a shame, this beautiful room and nobody using it, like the empty ball diamond I told you about.

She snapped out of it and said her name was Jean. I told her mine and shook her little toy hand.

"Enjoy your book," she said, and headed back.

Nice lady.

I sat down in a big sofa chair, put my feet up on a little footstool, and opened to page one.

Turns out there's a couple of other Aarons besides Henry.

There was one in the days of Moses—in fact, he was Moses's older brother. He was the founder of the Jewish priesthood and lived to be—ready for this?—a hundred and twenty-three years old. At my age he was only a third of the way through.

Then *Aaron, Henry*. All-time home run leader. But here's something surprising. He was a shortstop when he started out. That was in the Negro Leagues. It wasn't until the Braves got him that he became an outfielder. You can look it up.

The other Aaron was *Aaron ben Elijah*, but I closed my eyes for a minute and fell asleep . . .

I was down visiting my dad and it turned out his girlfriend Carlotta was really Jean the librarian. I could tell he was ashamed of how old and homely she was. We were all out walking around the desert and he was holding a ball of string tied to a button on her baggy dress. She kept trying to point out the different kinds of cactuses but he kept telling her to shut up. Then a breeze came and carried her into the air, going higher and higher while he let out all the string, till there she was, way the hell up in the sky, sprawling face down on the air with her dress spread out like a kite. "This is all I keep her for," he said. "The only reason." Then he gave me the string to hold while he lit a cigarette, but the string slipped through my fingers and she went up higher and higher until she was just a dot in the sky. And then the dot was gone.

It was horrible.

My dad kept patting my shoulder, saying, "It's all right. Don't worry about it. She was old. A hundred and twenty-three."

I woke up and it was Jean patting my shoulder.

"I'm sorry to wake you," she said, "but you kept crying out, so I thought perhaps I should."

I wasn't even embarrassed. I was just glad to see her back on the ground.

That evening, to show me my goal and inspire me towards it, I put that *Sport* magazine on my bed near the phone, open to the page with the picture of Nellie and his family, and tried calling Karen. But all I kept getting was her damn machine.

Between calls I did some serious housecleaning, which wore me out, being still pretty weak after my coma, and I wanted to turn in, so I decided to at least leave her a message. But I wanted to say it right, so I got a pen and paper. After a couple of rewrites, I had:

> *Hi Karen. Its Hank. Well, I took your advice and got up. I went to work yesterday and let me tell you it was sure good to be back. But enough about me. How have <u>you</u> been? Good, I hope. And how is that little rascal of yours doing? You know, I kind of miss the little fella. After all, he's basically a good kid. I was going to call you earlier but I was doing some research at the library and lost track of the time. Anyway I just wanted*

to say hello to you and Brian. I'll try again tomorrow after I return from the library. Goodnight, Karen. Goodnight, Brian.

I dialed again, held up the sheet of paper, cleared my throat—and wouldn't you know it, Karen answered, live.

I said, "Hi, Karen. It's Hank. Well, I took your advice and got up. I went to work yesterday and let me tell you—"

"That's good, Hank. Phil told me. I'm glad. What is it you wanted?"

"Well . . . nothing really. Just thought I'd give you a call. This a bad time?"

"Actually, yes. It is."

"What's the matter?"

"Nothing. Little situation with Brian."

"Want me to come over?"

"What for?"

"See if I can help out with the little rascal."

"The little what?"

"Rascal. After all, he's basically a good kid."

"No, he's not. And why are you talking so strange?"

"Am I?"

"Listen, I have to go."

"All right, but how about if I drop by tomorrow, after I return from the—"

"Brian! Gotta go. Bye."

She hung up.

"Goodnight, Karen. Goodnight, Brian."

If you're ever in southern Nigeria, make sure you visit the city of *Aba*, population 300,000. They've got just about everything, including their own brewery. And check out their world-renowned handicrafts.

They might even have restaurants serving *Abalone*, an edible one-shelled snail found in warm seas around the world. Their shells are often used in ornamental work.

Imagine eating *Abalone* in *Aba* while listening to music conducted by *Claudio Abbado*, who was born in Milan, Italy in 1937, and has a special interest in the music of Giocchino Rossini.

I looked up *Rossini, Giocchino* . . .

I walked over to Karen's tonight, but no one was home. So I sat on the deck stairs and waited. A nice night, lots of stars, a little breeze, and I was all showered and shaved, with plenty of Old Spice.

I started worrying, though. This being a Friday night, maybe she wasn't home because she was *with* someone, you know? Some guy, I mean. On a date. Having a wonderful time. Right this moment laughing at something he said, something clever as hell . . .

Or maybe . . .

I stood up.

Maybe right this moment . . .

By the time she pulled into the driveway I was pacing all over the lawn.

Turned out she'd only been to Jim's, her ex, dropping off Brian for the weekend.

She looked pretty tired but I talked her into sitting on the steps for a while, mentioning the stars and the little breeze.

"For a minute," she said.

I asked, "How's Brian?"

"Let's talk about something else."

"How's Jim?"

She shrugged. "He bought a pool table—sorry, a *billiard* table. He's all excited about it."

"Is that the kind with no holes?"

"No pockets."

"Right."

"Next week it'll be something else. One of those make-your-own-beer kits or something. He'll have it all set up on the pool table."

"Billiard table."

We sat there for a while not saying anything.

Then I asked her, "Have you ever eaten abalone?"

She asked me to repeat the question.

"Have you ever . . . eaten . . . abalone?"

"Abalone?"

"Right."

"Have I ever *eaten* it?"

"Right."

"No. Why?"

"Just wondering."

"I've *worn* it. I used to have an abalone necklace."

"Right—it *is* also used as an ornament."

"I didn't know it was something you ate."

"They're a shellfish, Karen."

She nodded.

I took her hand. She let me.

"They're found in warm seas around the world," I told her.

"Oh?"

We sat there holding hands.

"Ever hear of a man named Aaron?" I asked.

"The baseball player?"

"Nope."

We sat talking till pretty late. Not about us, though. We kind of avoided that topic. But we were holding hands throughout.

And I'll tell you something, I felt happy. I truly did. And *peace*ful, you know? Very peaceful and happy.

It had nothing to do with my plans for us—I mean about being Dad and Mom and the kids and all that. It just had to do with Karen, being with Karen, her hand in mine, the stars above.

I invited her to my game tomorrow. She said maybe.

Then we said goodnight. I made a move to kiss her and she gave me her cheek, but I was happy with that.

In fact, walking home, I was about as happy as I get.

2. Nobody said anything about last Saturday's game and my long crawl to the plate—nobody said anything to *me*, anyway. But Gordie had me sitting the bench.

I wouldn't have minded so much but Karen had come.

I could see her from the dugout, sitting out there in the stands in a little area by herself, a magazine open in her lap. She was wearing the Shopalot cap I gave her last year and this yellow dress I like which lets you see the freckles down her arms and above her boobs. She looked so damn nice I just kept standing there staring at her, thinking what a goddam fool I've been and hoping it wasn't too late.

Our team took the field, and when she saw I wasn't out there she looked towards the dugout.

I shrugged and turned up my hands.

She shrugged and went back to her magazine.

I took a seat.

It was just me and Gordie in there—Ross out talking to Officer Phil in his squad car and Brownie off buying Gordie a bag of sunflower seeds—so it could have been pretty awkward, considering the last time me and Gordie saw each other, but he was busy pacing back and forth, beating his hands, yelling, "Let's go! Let's go! Let's go! Let's go!"

Out on the mound Redman was standing very still with his arms at his sides, looking up at the bright blue sky, towards the Happy Hunting Ground or whatever. He stood like that for so long even Gordie finally shut up. Then he looked in for Burlson's sign, nodded his head, wound up very slowly . . . and *whoosh*, strike one.

Then *whoosh*, strike two.

And *whoosh*, strike three.

The batter looked like he was still waiting for the first pitch. Gordie yelled to him, "You can sit *down* now!"

The next guy at least struck out *swinging*.

The guy after that managed to nick a foul tip before *he* went down, too.

Everyone came charging back to the dugout, whooping it up, while Redman walked from the mound with big calm warrior strides.

Gordie was telling us, "Don't talk to him. Don't say a fucking word. Just leave him alone. Give him that end of the bench. Move, Lingerman. Go coach first base."

Little prick. I hadn't forgot those things he called me: Old. Pitiful. Loser.

I got up but I didn't go coach. I told Brownie to go. Then I did something I never did before in my whole career because I think it's bush league, but I didn't care:

I went out to visit with a fan.

"I guess one bench is as good as another," I said, sitting down next to Karen.

"Oh, well," she said.

I agreed. "No big deal." I looked around. "Beautiful day."

She thought so too.

I told her, "You look nice."

She thanked me.

I put it stronger: "Really nice."

She changed the subject. "*Bob* did good out there, didn't he?"

"Redman? Jesus, I guess."

She turned around to look at the rest of the stands, shading her eyes. "I don't see Janet."

"Well, no," I said, remembering how he talked to her on the phone the other night at my place.

Karen looked at me. "They having trouble?"

She went to high school with Janet.

I said, "Well, being married, there's bound to be a *little* trouble now and then. But I think if two people really, you know, care for each other? Really and truly care? Well—"

"What's Gordie trying to say?" she asked, changing the subject again.

He was in the third base coach's box, touching himself all over.

I said, "He's telling the batter that if two people really and truly—"

"Hank."

"He wants him to take the first pitch."

"Take it and what?"

"'Take' means let it go, don't swing at it."

"Why not?"

"Well, to see what the pitcher's got. Plus, Gordie just likes to give signals."

They had this long, loosey-goosey lefthander out there and he came straight overhand with a fastball down the middle of the plate and you could see it broke Mitch's heart to let it go.

"*Striiike!*" from the ump.

Gordie went into action again.

"What's he saying now?"

"He's saying, 'What's the *matter* with you, letting a pitch like that go by.'"

She elbowed me.

"He told him go ahead and swing away."

Which Mitchell did, lining a single into left.

"Good one," Karen said.

Then Dunbar stepped to the plate with his white shoes and his pants as tight as leotards and his neon wrist bands and batting gloves, plus the fucking bozo's wearing *sun*glasses.

"This is the guy instead of you, right?"

"Right."

"Are you hoping he doesn't do well?"

"No," I told her, and I meant it. You can't do that. You start doing that, you might as well quit.

"What's Gordie telling him?"

"Lay one down."

"One what."

"He wants him to bunt. Move the runner along."

"Sacrifice."

"There you go."

But Dunbar swung away, lifting a high pop foul behind home plate, and the catcher tossed off his mask, waltzed around under it, and made the catch.

We both looked over at Gordie.

He was standing with his hands on his hips watching Dunbar return to the dugout. Then he pointed to the bench and shouted, "Get real comfortable, 'cause that's where you're staying!" Then he looked around. "Where the hell's Lingerman?"

"Over here!" I held up my hand.

"Get in the damn dugout, will you?"

Karen wished me luck.

I decided now was the perfect moment.

I turned to her and said, "You know what would really help me to play my best? What would really inspire me?"

She didn't know.

I took her hand and looked her in the eye. "If you would agree to be my wife," I said.

She gave a sigh, not a romantic one, and took her hand back.

Out on the field I kept my eye on her in case she decided to leave, because if she did I would run right after her.

The first batter hit a grounder pretty far to my left and I got over there and grabbed the ball like it was a nuisance and fired it to first to get rid of him.

She clapped her hands politely.

The next guy whiffed.

The next guy popped out to Lavinski at first base, and I hurried back to her.

She told me nice play on the grounder.

I thanked her.

Then I said, "Speaking of great second basemen," and told her about looking through that old issue of *Sport* magazine the other night, with the article about Nellie Fox, and what interesting pictures it had, especially this one showing him and his wife and kids, and I described it to her. Then I gave a laugh and told her about this funny thing I did in my imagination, putting *my* head and hers and Brian's in place of theirs.

No response. Nothing. Not a word.

I said, "It didn't make a bad-looking picture, Karen." Then I sat there fussing with my glove, tightening the laces.

She finally spoke. "You know what this is?" She sounded mad. "You know why you want to marry me?"

"Well—"

She cut me off. "I'll *tell* you why." She looked around, and went on in a quieter voice. "You want to marry me because you've had your little . . . midlife crazy spell or whatever it was and now you want to go ahead and be a grownup family man, like your hero, and you want *me* to be the wife in the picture because . . . basically because I'm *here*, you already know me, I already have a kid—I'm like a—like a family *starter*-kit." She looked me in the eye. "See what I'm saying, Hank?"

I saw. But I wanted to tell her about last night, how I felt sitting on the porch with her, and how I felt afterwards walking home. How happy. And how I felt when I saw her here today, in her yellow dress. But I had this hard little ball in my throat, so I all I did was shrug, looking down into my glove, and a big fat fucking tear plopped into the pocket.

"Hank . . ."

I shook my head, meaning No pity please, no thank you, and shook loose another goddam tear.

From out on the field I heard *ping* but didn't look.

"Good catch out there," she reported.

Still looking into my glove I said to her, "The thing is, Karen . . ."

But she didn't want to hear about it and went on doing the play-by-play: "Two outs now. Number eighteen the batter. Tall drink of water. Doesn't look too confident, though."

Fitz.

"Pitcher throws the ball, batter swings, hits it up in the air, not very far, and a guy catches it. Three outs."

"The thing is, I love you," I said, still looking into my glove. "And it's got nothing to do with Nellie Fox."

She was quiet.

I tightened the laces on my glove some more.

"I think you're supposed to be out there," she said.

"I don't care," I told her. And I didn't.

We sat there.

Gordie yelled, "Lingerman!"

I got up.

The goddam laces on my glove were pulled so tight I could barely get my hand in there, but it didn't matter since the first batter popped out to third and the next two went down swinging.

A couple of times during the inning Karen seemed to be looking at me, *staring* at me. But I wasn't sure.

The top of our order was up when we went in to hit, meaning I was up second, so I couldn't go talk to her. But I could speak to her with my bat. So instead of grabbing my wooden club I selected one of these whippy, skinny-handled metal jobs, wanting to launch the ball out of sight, wanting to make her gasp.

Mitchell grounded to short but the guy threw it away and Mitch trotted to second, representing the go-ahead run, the score still zip-zip.

As I walked towards the plate Gordie started screaming my name. I looked and he went through the bunt signal but in a very exaggerated way and even made a little bunting motion—I guess the idea being they'll think he's trying to make them think we're going to bunt and so they'll think we're really not, but then we will, or some such shit.

I stepped into the batter's box.

"Lingerman!"

He erased the bunt signal.

It didn't matter either way because, like I said, I'd made up my mind I was gonna crank one, fuck the bunt, or this little poke-hitting shit I always do. I wanted to show her some brute manly power, and held the bat down at the end, waving the head around—menacingly, as they say.

The pitcher being a southpaw and me a lefthanded batter, I was looking for a breaking ball—but not such a *nasty* one. Swing and a miss, strike one.

Lots of hooting and hollering from the infield.

Fine. I dug in closer to the plate and a full step further up in the box. Let him try that again. Come on . . .

But instead he came high and hard, the ball tailing in, straight for my face, and for a moment I froze—

Now she'll be sorry!

—but I got the bat up in time as I fell backwards, with a very silly-assed result, the ball hitting the bat—*ping*—and sailing right back to the mound.

But I heard Karen yell, "*Hank*," like I'd been hit.

And then I did something I'm ashamed to tell. I laid there, like she was right, like I'd been hit.

The ump declared fair ball, batter's out, so *he* knew it hit my bat, but I stayed the way I was, on my back, arms spread, eyes closed, wanting to scare her.

I figured I'd lay there for maybe ten or fifteen seconds, then kind of wake up and go staggering back to the dugout. And meanwhile she'd be feeling all these deep things and realize she still loved me and decide to say, *Yes, I'll marry you, Hank.*

But I didn't expect her to come running out onto the *field.*

I'm not lying, she came running over and knelt down beside me in the dirt, yellow dress and all, and put her hand on my cheek.

"Hank?" she said.

I opened my eyes a little and blinked, like waking up.

And I'll tell you something. The way she was looking down at me? I knew I was right. I mean about her still loving me.

I gave her my hand to hold.

Meanwhile, Gordie was all over the umpire, telling him he was out of his mind, the ball didn't hit the bat, it hit the batter, just *look* at me there, and so on.

I said to Karen in a weak, faraway voice, "Will you . . . marry me?" And gave a little cough.

But before she could answer, the umpire told me to get my ass up and off the playing area right now or we would forfeit for delay of game.

Gordie told me, "Come on," and gave my foot a little kick. "Good try. Both of you."

I let go of her hand. I said, "Karen, I'm sorry," and got up.

She stayed kneeling there, looking up at me with her mouth open.

"You too, lady," the umpire told her. "Let's go."

She left the ballpark. I let her go. Forever, I figured.

As far as the game, Mancini that inning drove Mitchell home with a single to right, which turned out to be all the scoring we needed, Redman achieving one of the rarest things in baseball: a perfect game. Twenty-seven batters up, twenty-seven batters down.

The last out was a strikeout and everyone went running up to the mound—but the way Redman was standing there with his arms in the air, bellowing all that Hey-ah, wey-ah stuff at the sky, they left him alone and just congratulated each other—high-fives and slaps on the ass, and so on. I didn't take part in it. I was too unhappy. I just walked to my car and drove home.

Karen was there, lying on the couch in her yellow dress, fast asleep.

3. When I told George I was getting married he said, "Nawww."

I said, "Yes, sir."

He told me to wait there and went to his office and came back with two big brown cigars.

"So what's this poor unfortunate woman's name?"

"Karen. You've met her. Karen Spaulding."

"Well, *sure*. Fact, she's the one I called, looking for you."

"Right. While I was . . ."

"In your coma, yeah. She told me you were out of the picture, completely."

"Well, that was then."

"And this is now. You set a date?"

"Not yet."

"These are from Cuba, by the way."

"Like Minnie Minoso."

"That's it."

I said, "Y'know, it's a goddam *crime* that that man is not in the Hall of Fame."

George laughed. "You're very happy, aren't you."

I told Jean.

I was at *Alexander the Great*, 356-323 BC, King of Macedonia, conqueror of the Persian Empire, and went out and asked her where those places were.

She likes when I ask her things.

She took me over to a globe on one of the tables. This old wino, Rudy, was reading a newspaper nearby, so we kept our voices down.

"Alexander's Macedonia was this area here, in northern Greece," she told me, tapping a little pink place. "And the ancient Persian Empire, well, that included what is now . . . let's see . . ."

"I'm getting married," I said quietly.

She looked up at me. "Sorry?"

Kind of a strange response.

I told her, "Not at all. Why? You think I *should* be?"

She looked confused. "Should be what?"

"*Sorry*," I said.

She blinked. "Regarding . . . ?"

"Well, she has this kid."

She shook her head, like she still wasn't following me.

"From her first marriage," I explained. "His name's Brian."

Rudy said, "Hey. Shh."

I whispered to Jean, "Go ahead. You were saying. Alexander? The Great?"

"Yes. Well . . ." She turned kind of slowly back to the globe. "Let's see . . ."

But I couldn't let go of it. "He thinks his daddy's God

Almighty," I whispered, "and here's his mom with this grease monkey. See what I'm saying?"

She turned on me. "No, I *don't*. What in the world are you *talking* about?"

"About *Brian*."

"Quiet!" Rudy told us.

Jean asked me in a pissed-off whisper, "Who is Brian?"

"Her kid."

"Whose kid?"

"Karen's."

"And who is Karen?"

"My fiancee."

She looked surprised. "You're getting married?"

Jean is a very intelligent person but she's also pretty old and I guess sometimes the blood doesn't get all the way up there or something.

I told her yes, as of Saturday.

"Is that what . . ."

"I been trying to tell you, yeah."

"Well, that's . . . *won*derful, Hank." She touched my arm. "Congratulations."

"Thanks. He's not really a *bad* kid."

"This is . . . ?"

"Brian. I mean, he's not evil."

"Oh, I'm sure he's not. How old is he?"

"Ten. He really does despise me, though."

"Well, it's a very difficult adjustment for a child that age to make—an *enormous* adjustment."

I liked that idea. Brian didn't *really* despise me. He was just having trouble adjusting. Which was only natural. I mean, after all, it wasn't some *little* adjustment.

I said, "You're right. It's an *enormous* adjustment."

Rudy said, "How 'bout adjusting your goddam voices? I'm tryna *read* here."

We both apologized.

I whispered to Jean, "The Persian Empire. Show me."

My suspension at the Palace was up, so after the library I stopped by to share my news.

Tommy was there, with Mancini and Burlson and Fitz, Larry behind the bar, and a couple guys I didn't know playing pool.

Soon as I walked in Tommy said, "Hear the news?"

It was about Redman. He beat up Janet last night and she called 911. He was sitting right now in jail.

Tommy got it from Officer Phil, who was one of the cops that went over there. He told Tommy there was blood on her face and her front tooth was broke and she kept screaming, "Get him out of here!" He said Redman was sitting on the couch and didn't say a word while they cuffed him and took him away.

"I wish to fuckin' Christ I coulda seen her get it," Tommy said. "This was long, long overdue."

Burlson said it depends how he hit her. "If he punched her up, which it sounds like he did, well, that's wrong. *Open* hand.

Always open hand. A good hard slap in the face can say just as much—say it better, in fact."

Mancini disagreed. "The best thing to do when you're itching to hit her is just get out of the house, just get the hell away from her." He said that's what he was doing here tonight.

Fitz said there was no possible way he could ever hit a woman.

Tommy said, "There's no possible way you could ever fuck one either."

That broke everyone up, even the pool players.

Fitz muttered something about Vanna White.

Tommy said, "What was that? What was that?"

Larry jumped in, "Here ya go. Listen to this," and started reading out loud about a butcher in Berlin who made sausage links out of his wife.

I decided to go see Tony with my happy news.

On the way there, I thought about whether I could ever hit Karen.

I tried to imagine slapping her face, like Burlson recommends.

I couldn't.

But maybe Redman couldn't imagine hitting Janet.

I tried to imagine slapping *Brian's* face.

It was easy. There's his face, here's my hand: Slap.

Slap.

Slap.

I sat in the little empty bar off the dining area waiting for Tony to notice me. I figured we'd both be a little embarrassed, since the last time we saw each other I was in my coma and he was ranting about the little worms on the sidewalk. But when he came in he yelled, "Hey! Stromboli Van Winkle!" and drew me a beer and himself one too. "Good to see you back in action."

As he set my glass down I said to him, "Tony, I would like to share some good news with you"—like that, kind of formal, maybe because of his tuxedo. "Karen Spaulding and I . . ." But then I wondered. "*You* know Karen, right?"

"Your old girl friend."

"Right."

"She's the one called me when you were . . . you know . . ."

"In bed, right. Anyway—"

"Hey, tell me something. You get up on your own? Or somebody talk you into it?"

"You mean who won the bet?"

"Well . . . yeah. But you know, Stromboli, I was coming to see you anyway."

"That's all right."

"So who won?"

"I'm not sure. I think Gordie did. It was kind of—"

"You got up for *that* little—"

"Hey, I didn't get up for *any*one, okay? I got up for my—" But then I remembered. "Actually, I got up for Tommy."

"But he didn't want you up."

"He needed a ride home."

"And that's what you got up for? So you could do that asshole a favor?" He shook his head. "Stromboli."

"What."

"Go back to bed."

That hurt. It really did.

I said, "Fine. Goodnight," and stood up and pulled out my wallet.

"Hey. *Kidding*. Come on. Sit down. *Sit*," he told me.

I sat.

"So sensitive, this guy."

I shrugged.

"You were telling me something. About you and this Karen. What is it. You back together?"

"We're getting married."

Tony went Italian.

"Dio mio!" he said, then reached over and grabbed my head in his hands and planted a big kiss on my forehead.

"Hey! Jesus!" I wiped it off.

He picked up his beer and held it out: "*Salut*."

I picked up mine.

"To you and Karen. Happiness of all types and kinds," he said, really meaning it.

I told him, "Thanks, Tony."

We drank to me and Karen and happiness of all types and kinds.

"That's a very nice lady," he said.

"I know."

"You're a lucky motherfucker, Stromboli."

I agreed.

"A lucky motherfucker."

I agreed again.

"Some people aren't so lucky," he said.

"Oh?"

I knew what was coming.

"Like this friend of mine," he said, and launched into one of his jokes about a guy out looking for pussy.

I sipped my beer and waited for the punch line.

"So you know what he did?" he finally said.

"No. What'd he do?" I got set to laugh.

"You really wanna hear what he did?"

"Sure. Go ahead."

"I'll tell you what he did, he went home and fucked his wife, what the hell." He drank down his beer.

I didn't get it.

But I went ahead and laughed anyway: "Ah ha ha . . ."

Tony shook his head. "Stromboli."

"What."

"You laugh about as good as you snore."

I didn't get that, either.

I gave my dad a call.

"Hello, who's there?"

"Hey, Whitey."

"Well, for Chrissake."

"Listen up. I got some good news. I'm getting married."

He didn't say anything.

"Dad?"

No response.

I got scared. "Hey. *Dad.*"

"Hank," he said, "I'm standing here and I got tears . . . I got tears running right down my face. That's how happy I am."

"Well . . ."

"And sad, Hank. Sad, too."

"Why sad?"

"Think about it."

"Mom, you mean?"

"But wait until I tell her. She'll flip, Hank. She really will."

"She probably already knows, wouldn't you think?"

"You're right. Of course she knows. Wait until I see her. We'll have something to talk about for a change. Who's the girl? Wait'll I tell Carlotta. She'll be thrilled, Hank. I've told her all about you. She's here right now, out on the porch. We just ate a late supper. She made enchilladas. Holy Christ, can that woman cook. I'm telling ya, Hank, she's got it all. So who's the girl?"

"Karen. Karen Spaulding?"

"Sure. With the . . ."

"Kid. Yeah."

"Little boy, isn't it?"

"Right."

"How old's he?"

"Ten."

"You get along?"

"Well . . ."

"Because I'll tell you something, Hank, it's a tough job bringing up a kid. Believe me, I know. You were no picnic. Baseball. That's all that mattered to you. Never mind school work. Never mind helping your mom around the house. Never mind making your old man happy—like maybe taking over for him when he's ready to retire. No. Baseball. That's all that counted. And look at you now, Hank. Working for a nigger. You know how that makes me feel? Do you have any idea how that makes me feel?"

"Dad, listen, it's starting to rain and I think—"

"So when's this gonna happen? When's the big day?"

"We haven't set a date yet. Soon as we do, though—"

"Y'know, I knew damn well you weren't queer. I was telling Carlotta, after you called me about your friend— whats his name again?"

"His name? It's . . ." I couldn't remember.

"How's he doing, by the way?"

"Good. He finally got up."

"Glad to hear it. I was telling Carlotta, and you know what she said? How could any son of *mine* be queer? 'Not posseeble.' she says, like that. 'Not posseeble.'"

"Right. Listen, I gotta go now, Dad. I'll let you know when we set a date. If you could come, that would be—"

"What the hell you mean, 'if'? Of *course* I'll be there. I'm your goddam father, for Chrissake."

"And Carlotta, too. She's invited."

"Well, we'll see. She's . . . pretty busy these days. But we'll see."

"All right, Dad. Well, good talking to you."

"Hank?"

"Yeah?"

"I'm proud of you."

"Thanks, Dad."

"Car windows up?"

"All the way."

"Attaboy."

"Bye, Dad."

"So long, Hank."

I went to the bathroom and blew my nose.

Karen had Brian in bed asleep before I got there, so we kept our voices down, sitting together on the couch. I asked her if she told him yet about us getting married.

"No. I will, though. Soon."

"But he knows we're . . . together again, right?"

"Actually, no, I haven't told him that yet, either."

"Well, *Jesus*, Karen."

"Shh."

"Well, Jesus," I whispered.

"Let's see if there's a movie on," she said. "All right?"

Sometimes Karen just wants to watch a movie.

She found an old one, in black and white, with Humphrey Bogart.

I asked her did she hear about Redman.

She nodded. "Phil was by."

"Man, I'll tell you something—"

"Let's just watch, hon, okay?" she said, snuggling up.

So that's what we did.

"Sure smoked enough back then, didn't they?" I said.

"Uh huh."

I rested my eyes for a minute . . .

Next thing I know she's waking me up and helping me to my feet. "Let's go, mister. Movie's over. Take it home."

I went staggering off towards the bedroom, unbottoning my shirt.

"Bad idea, Hank," she said, following me.

"C'mon, I'm outa here by seven. He's never up."

"I know but—"

"I'll be extra quiet. Won't make a sound. Don't worry. Shhh . . ."

And the next thing I know after that, *Brian's* waking me, standing by the bed in the dark poking my shoulder, going, "Mom, I had a nightmare. Can I get in?"

This kid is ten years old.

He poked me harder. "Mom?"

"Other side," I told him.

He stepped back and just stood there a moment—stunned, I guess. Then he started yelling, "Mom! Mom! Mom!"

Karen was out of bed and in her robe and over there like *that*. She brought him into the living room, Brian wanting to know, "Was that *him*? Was that *him*?"

"Yes."

"But you said! You promised! No more Hank!"

"Brian . . ."

"You promised! You promised! You—"

"Stop it."

'No! I hate you! I hate your guts!"

"Listen to me, Brian, all right? Just—"

"Fuck you!"

Fuck you? I got up and found my pants. But then I thought, No. Stay out of it.

So I stood there in the dark listening to him call his mother a liar and a bitch and a big stupid fat ugly pig. When I finally heard his bedroom door slam I put my pants on and went out there.

She was sitting on the edge of the couch, hands in her lap, gazing straight ahead.

I sat down carefully beside her.

"My fault," I said.

She shrugged.

You could hear Brian in his room, wailing away.

Still staring off, she said, "It's not too late, Hank."

To back out of marrying her, she meant.

I took her hand from her lap and told her it was *way* too late.

We sat there holding hands, listening to Brian.

I said, "This is a big adjustment for a child his age to make."

She looked at me.

"An e*normous* adjustment," I said.

She laid her forehead against my arm. I thought she was crying, the way her shoulders were shaking. But she wasn't crying.

4. After work today I stopped by the Palace before heading to the library, to see if there was any news about Redman.

I was in jail once myself—just overnight, but it was a long damn night. This was down in Springfield, Virginia, after I'd gotten the pink slip that ended my minor league career.

Funny thing is, it was after a game I'd gotten a pair of hits, one of them a double. But as I walked into the locker room I noticed everyone turning away, pretending to be busy with buttons or shoe laces. And when I got to my locker I saw why.

It really *is* a pink slip.

It said to go see Benny, our manager, in his office. So I did and he told me how much he'd like to keep me, that I was helping the team, but he said since the whole point of the minors is to develop talent for the parent club and since I was too old for any future up *there* . . .

I got out of there before I started crying. I was still in my uniform but I didn't want to go back to the locker room until everyone was gone, so I walked out to the field, into the third base dugout, and laid on the bench and cried like a child. Cried myself to sleep, in fact.

When I woke up, the lights were off, the sky was full of stars, and all was quiet. I sat there for a while, trying to say goodbye.

I finally just said, "Well, goodbye."

The locker room was this little concrete building near the street and by now it was all locked up. There were windows above the showers but I couldn't reach them, so I went back to the field—kind of embarrassed after already saying goodbye—and dragged this little backstop on wheels over to one of the windows and climbed up, but it was locked. So I got down and moved the backstop to the next one. But then a cop car pulls up and this young hardass gets out, going, "What the *hell* you think *you're* doing?"

I probably could have explained, but at the moment I was pretty aggravated, on top of feeling sort of grief-stricken at being released. Plus, being still in my uniform, near the ballfield, I was seeing him as more of an umpire than a cop, and I started giving him hell, right up in his face, going, "Whaddaya think, I'm a *thief*? I'm a *ball*player, okay? I be*long* here. So you blew *that* one, buddy. You blew *that* one."

He had me across the hood of the car and cuffed real quick. Real tight, too.

The worst part was, I ended up in a cell with some guy on speed or something, who wouldn't let me sleep. All night he went on about *his* playing days—mostly softball, slow-pitch.

Anyway, guess who was sitting at the bar all by himself getting loaded.

Redman.

He said he was glad to see me out of bed, and I told him I was glad to see him out of jail.

Janet had dropped the charges. But he didn't want to go home, couldn't face her.

He looked like hell.

I sat on the next stool and said, "Well . . ."

Larry brought me a glass of Old Style and returned to his ash tray and the *National Enquirer*.

Redman said he was thinking very seriously about taking off, heading west, maybe out around South Dakota. "Sioux country. My people. My *kin nipi*. That means relatives. Go out there, live in a tent or something."

"Teepee, you mean."

"Maybe hook up with a shaman."

"A what?"

"A shaman. A medicine man. A spiritual guide."

"Like a priest, you mean."

"Fuck, like a priest. I'm talking about *wochangi*, man. You know what that is?"

"Not really."

"Wochangi's like . . . it's like . . . I'll show you." He sat up straight and closed his eyes and started doing that "hey-ah, wey-ah" shit, which I didn't feel like hearing, and I said to him, "Wait. *Red*man. Yo!"

He stopped. "What."

"How 'bout some coffee? Now *there's* an old Indian drink."

He didn't want any coffee and took a pull on his bottle of Heineken, then told me some more about going out to South Dakota and hanging out with a medicine man, maybe being his assistant, driving him around to his clients, doing little chores for him.

"You could do his taxes."

I was just kidding, but he shook his head and told me Indians don't have to file.

Larry looked up from his newspaper. "You're shittin' me."

Redman leaned closer to me. "Know what I would *really* like? To be more than his assistant. To be his ap*prentice*. You know? The person he passes all his knowledge and wisdom to." He went into this medicine man voice: "'Listen to my words. Here is the sacred way, my son.' That's what he would call me: 'My son.' And I'd call him Grandfather.' I'd say, 'Yes, Grandfather. I am listening.'" He poked my arm, hard. "*That's* what I'd like," he said, and returned to his beer.

I wondered how serious he was about all this. So I told him that sounded like a pretty good idea.

He looked at me. "You think so?"

I shrugged. "Like you said, those are your people."

"Yeah, but I mean . . . just *go*?"

"Well, I'd tell Janet first."

He told Larry to bring him another Heinekin and a shot of C.C. along with it. Then he sat there folding and creasing a paper napkin. "I broke her tooth. Did you know that?"

"That's what I heard."

He seemed to be concentrating really hard on folding that napkin just so. Then he put his hands over his face and started crying.

I thought about patting his shoulder. But I don't like touching guys. And anyway he *should* feel bad, what the hell.

Larry very carefully set the shot and beer in front of him and carefully returned to his spot, practically on tiptoes.

Redman went on crying.

I sipped my beer.

After a minute he sat up straight and ran his sleeve across his eyes. Then he picked up his shot, drank it down in one toss and chased it with a long drink of beer, belched and said, "Pardon."

I hate to say this but I was kind of wishing I could leave him with some good advice, then head for the library, for my chair and my book.

He started going on about his Perfect Game.

"Honest to God, Hank, after that last out? I didn't wanna leave the mound. I didn't wanna come *down* from there. Greatest fucking moment of my life, standing up there doing my victory song. Giving praise and thanks to my ancestors. Because, see, they were with me, man. That whole game, they were out there with me. I mean, how else, you know? How else could I have done what I did? Twenty-seven batters. Think about it. Twenty-seven fucking batters. They all came *up*, and they all . . . went . . . *down*," slamming his fist on the bar. "Per*fection*, man. Per*fection*!"

I told him I thought Burlson caught a good game—because the catcher should always get some of the credit. I also thought he might have mentioned a couple of pretty handy plays Yours Truly made out there on balls that could have gone through for hits, and there goes his Perfection, man.

But he just kept going on about not wanting to come down from the mound, not ever.

Tommy came in. "*Ton*to. Hey. See ya got my cake with the file. *That's* good." He came over and put his hand on Redman's shoulder and said to him sincerely, "How you doing? You doing okay?" Then he goes, "Christ, you smell worse than Chicklit here," and laughed and gave Redman's shoulder a shake, Redman being his hero now, not for the Perfect Game but for belting Janet.

Tommy hates all women except for his mother and Vanna White, although with Vanna it's kind of complicated and sometimes he hates her worse than any woman alive.

"Lemme buy you a beer," he said.

Redman said, "What the hell for?" and pulled his shoulder away from Tommy's hand, like he knew what for.

"Fuck-ya, then," Tommy told him, and walked back to his usual stool, his feelings hurt. He told Larry to bring him a draft and get the TV on. "Let's go."

Redman downed the rest of his beer and shoved back his stool. "Here's what I'll say: 'I'm sorry, Jan. Sorry about your tooth, sorry about everything. I'm gonna go to South Dakota now and learn how to become a better human being. I don't know when I'll be back.'" He stood up, not too steadily.

I asked him if he wanted me to drive him.

His eyes got big. "You wanna come? That's *great*, Hank. Listen, that ceremony we did at your place, that was bullshit, that was fake. But out *there*, man—"

"I meant drive you home, to your house."

"Oh," he said. "I thought . . ." He sighed. "Nah. Thanks. I'll walk. Clear my head."

"Good idea," I told him.

"Get up, man, so I can hug you," he said.

"That's okay." I held out my hand to shake.

He took it and pulled me up off the stool and gave me a bear hug, pinning my arms to my sides. "You're all right, Hank. You know that? For a white man."

I told him he was all right for a red man.

"Ya fuckin' homo!" Tommy yelled. "Go back to the slammer if you wanna do that shit!"

His feelings were still hurt.

Back in my book I jumped ahead to the letter *S* and took a look at *South Dakota:* The Coyote State. First belonged to France. U.S. bought it in 1803 as part of Louisiana Purchase. (Redman would probably say, First belonged to the Indians and still does.) Became a state in 1889. Economic opportunities have remained limited. Famous site: Mount Rushmore.

Those heads. One is Washington. One is Lincoln . . .

I went out and asked Jean about the others.

Thomas Jefferson and Theodore Roosevelt.

I asked her what she knew about Indian medicine men.

She went on for a while.

I asked her if they took apprentices.

"Oh, absolutely."

"Would they take a white person, you think?"

She looked at me funny. "Are you getting cold feet, Hank?"

It took me a moment.

"*No,*" I said. "It's a friend of mine. He's . . . thinking about a career change."

"I see."

"No. Seriously."

Tell you what, though. I didn't really think Redman would actually go. He was just drunk, I figured. When I was drunk I sometimes used to talk about going to Japan and playing for the Tokyo Giants and having my own little geisha girl. Sometimes I even talked about it when I *wasn't* drunk. Japanese women are so beautiful.

But he wasn't at our game the next night and nobody knew where he was. Officer Phil was there, in his squad car out beyond the third base bleachers, and even he didn't know. He said he'd swing by Redman's house, though, and investigate.

Gordie was a mess because here we were, three games to go, tied for first place with the Hounds, and the guy who's mostly made it possible has gone missing. He waited as long as he could before turning in his line-up card, with Fitzgerald down as our starting pitcher.

Fitz promised to do his best.

Gordie said, "Fine," sitting there copying down the other team's line-up: the Ace Hardware Aces.

"That's all I can do," Fitz added. "I mean, that's all *any*one can do, right? Their best. You know?"

"Yep."

"Can't make any promises."

Gordie nodded.

"No guarantees," Fitz told him.

"All right."

"Except just one, and you know what that is? That one guarantee?"

Gordie looked up from his scorebook. "Will ya let me do this? Go bother Brownie."

But Brownie was out on the field kissing up to one of the umps, so Fitz came over to me. He said there was only one thing he could guarantee when he went out on that mound tonight and asked me if I knew what it was.

I took a wild guess. "You'll do your best?"

He pointed at me. "You got it, pal."

Fitz walked the first three batters he faced and Gordie sent him out to right field and brought in Brannigan. The Bran Man gave up a two-run single but then retired the next three batters.

I watched all this from the bench, Dunbar out there at second base.

Which I tried to be big about. I really did. I even gave him some advice the next inning after he blew a routine grounder.

I was trying to follow Nellie's example in 1964 when he tutored the rookie Joe Morgan, even though Morgan was taking his job away. Fox turned him into a Golden Glove second baseman. And it was good to read what Morgan said at his Hall of Fame induction ceremony last spring, mentioning Nellie's generous help and how grateful he would always be.

I told Dunbar, "On a grounder like that, don't wait for it. Charge the ball. Read the hops and get a clean one. Don't let the ball play *you*, know what I mean?"

He looked at me. "You got some shit on your chin," he said.

Tobacco juice.

Later that same inning Officer Phil entered the dugout and announced that he had an announcement to make concerning the whereabouts of Redman.

Gordie came in from the coach's box to hear.

Phil said he had just spoken with Redman's wife, who informed him that Redman had departed from home last evening in his vehicle, a white BMW, heading in the general direction of South Dakota, with the stated intention of setting up residence on an Indian reservation.

He said that was all the information he had at this time. He wished us luck, told us to play hard but play fair, and left the dugout.

"Play with this," Gordie said, giving his crotch a shake, and slumped onto the bench.

Karen showed up around the fourth inning—with Brian. A first. She must have bribed him. He hates baseball. He actually told me that once. Said he hates the game. "It's so *boring*," he said, and started chanting: "*Bor*-ing, *bor*-ing, *bor*-ing . . ."

Whenever I looked over there tonight he was hunched over his Game Boy, this little electronic thing he takes whenever he has to be somewhere he doesn't want to be.

He missed a pretty exciting ballgame. We lost, 3-2. We were down 2-1 in the top of the ninth when Fitzgerald, of all people, tied it for us with a two-out single to right, sending Mancini home and Burlson to third with the possible go-ahead run.

But then Fitz takes his lead-off and the first baseman says to him, "Nice hit, buddy," and Fitz begins telling him about trying to do your best, how that's all you can do, and the first baseman agrees and takes the pickoff throw and tags him out.

I was coaching first base at the time, so it was my fault too.

Thing is, by that point I was having trouble keeping my head in the game, after sitting the bench all that time. I kept catching myself staring up at this big white full moon, thinking about things, mostly about Redman out there driving around South Dakota looking for a medicine man, looking for help, which maybe I coulda gave him yesterday in the bar—except, what the hell do I know? Not much, besides baseball and a little bit of the encyclopedia, up to *Ascorbic acid*, which is Vitamin C, found in fresh fruits and vegetables.

Anyway, that's what I was doing in the coach's box, moon gazing, when Fitz got nabbed. I threw up my hands and told him, "*Wake up, will ya?*"

Then, in the bottom of the inning, their first batter ended the game, driving a Brannigan fastball into the darkness beyond center field.

I grabbed my unused glove and left the dugout.

Gordie was sitting there going, "Thanks a lot, Redman. Thanks a whole fucking lot . . ."

I stood talking with Karen in the parking lot for a while, mostly about Redman's departure. Brian took her keys and got in the car and went on with his Game Boy.

"Tell him yet?"—about us getting married, I meant.

"No, but I will—*okay*? "

When Karen says *Okay?* like that, she means *Back off*, so I changed the subject, asking her how she got Brian to come to the game.

"One medium-sized Hawaiian pizza at Antonio's tomorrow night." She touched my arm. "Why don't you meet us there?"

"I got a better idea. Why don't we all go together?" I said.

She made a face. "I think that might be pushing it a little."

So let's push, I wanted to say.

"We'll be there around seven," she went on. "Just come over to our table like . . ."

"'Fancy meeting *you* here'?"

"Right."

"Karen . . ."

"I know, I know," she said, not wanting to hear.

So we said goodnight. She gave me a quick little kiss—but I put my arms around her: my big beautiful bride-to-be.

"All right, honey," she said, patting my back, wanting to break this up, with Brian around.

But let him see, you know? He *should* see. And I went on holding her, tight. "So when you wanna get married?" I said.

"Hank . . ."

"A week?" I said. "A month?"

"Let *go* of me."

"A year?"

It was probably a good thing Brian started laying on the horn.

Part Four

Brian

My own mother tricked me bad.

She said if I went to Hank's baseball game she would take me the next night for pizza. I hate baseball and I hate Hank but I did it, I went. So the next night we're sitting in Antonio's, we already ordered, we got our Cokes with the clear straws and the little ice cubes, we're taking the quiz on the place mats, everything's fine, then guess who comes walking over—*because they already planned it.*

"Hey there!" he goes.

And she goes, "Well, hi!"

Like what a surprise.

Then he sits right down in the other chair.

I was so mad I almost started crying, but I didn't. I just slid way down and sucked on my Coke.

He starts going, "Hey, what happened to Brian? Where'd he go?"—looking all around for me.

Funny old Hank.

Before, all he practically ever said was hi, but now he keeps trying to make me *like* him, and I know why. So I'll want him to be my new dad and he can marry my mom and we'll be this little family, instead of him living by himself in his grody little apartment where he belongs.

The waitress came and he told her a bottle of beer and a roast beef sandwich. She asked me if I wanted another Coke. I was down to just ice but I shook my head.

Not if *he* was paying. Which he probably was. Trying to be the big Father.

I slunked down even more and stared at a bunch of blue grapes hanging over the door all the way on the other side of the room while he told my mom this totally boring story all about some guy and his car.

I wish I could live with my dad.

He's a lawyer. He's got an office with a picture of him and George Bush on his desk. My dad's smiling real casual like it's no big deal but George Bush is smiling real hard like *he's* the one it's a big deal for, getting his picture taken with my dad.

Know what my dad calls Hank? He calls him Goober. It's from this real old dorky TV show, *Andy Griffith*. Ever see it? There's this guy named Goober, and him and Hank are exactly alike. They both work in a gas station and they're both real grubby and ugly and low class and dumb.

The waitress came back with a cart and put Goober's beer and sandwich down in front of him and my mom's salad in front of her and my pizza with sausage and black olives and pineapple in front of me but I just stayed the way I was and didn't even look. I could smell it, though, being nose-level with the table.

Soon as the waitress left, my mom said, "Brian?"

I kept staring at those grapes I told you about.

"Hon, sit up and eat."

It was hard to tell if they were real grapes or rubber.

She tried getting tough. "Brian, sit up right now and eat your pizza."

I figured they were probably rubber, the way they looked too perfect.

"C'mon, man."

That was Goober.

So now I'm staring away in a complete total trance like a complete total zombie. Ever see *Night of the Living Dead*?

I heard my mom give a big sigh. I heard Goober take a gulp of beer.

Then Tony the owner came over in his white tuxedo.

I thought it was maybe because I wasn't eating, but he came up behind Goober and shook him by the shoulders and called him Rippa Vanna Winkle and they all laughed, whoever Rippa Vanna Winkle was.

Then he said to my mom, "I wanna to wish-a you congratulations on-a you happy news."

She said, "*Thank* you," and started telling him what a delicious salad, how fresh, and what great dressing, even though she didn't even take a bite yet.

He said, "Grazie, grazie."

What happy news?

Then Tony looked over at me. "So whatsa *you* problem?"

I shrugged.

"You no like-a you pizza?"

I shrugged.

"You no even *try* it. Sit up and-a eat."

I sat up. I mean, he's the owner.

He watched me take a bite. They all watched.

Tony goes, "Not-a so bad, eh? Better than rat-a poison? Maybe?"

I shrugged—still not swallowing, though. Soon as he left I was gonna spit it out.

"Nice-a boy," he said to my mom.

"Mm," she said.

Then he told us, "On-a the house. My treat. Enjoy," and took off.

So Goober wasn't paying for it now.

I went ahead and swallowed.

He stayed overnight and I couldn't sleep, thinking about him touching her.

I got up and tossed in my T-2 video, with the sound down low. *Terminator 2: Judgment Day*, my favorite movie of all time. Seen it?

It's got excellent violence and stuff but you know what's my favorite scene? Where the kid John Connor and Arnold Schwarzenegger, the Terminator—which is a cyborg from the future—are goofing around together, giving each other high and low fives and stuff, and John's mother says, "The Terminator would never leave him. And it would die to protect him. Of all the would-be fathers, this machine was the only one who measured up. In an insane world, it was the sanest choice."

I always feel like I'm gonna start crying when she says all that, me being like John Connor, no father around and stuff. Except *he's* got Arnold Schwarzenegger for a fill-in, and what've I got? Goober.

Sometimes I like to think about the Terminator showing up on his motorcycle and we go off together.

But before we do, there's this scene where I'm sitting on the back of his chopper with my arms around him while my mom and my dad are both begging me to stay and they even promise to get back together again. But I tell them, "In an insane world, this is the sanest choice." Then Arnie guns the engine and we peel away.

But then Hank starts chasing us in his crappy little car, trying to impress my mom as usual, and he's gaining on us but Arnie pulls out his sawed-off shotgun and turns around and yells, "Hasta la vista, baby!" and pulls the trigger and I don't even want to describe what happens to Hank's whole face.

Then there's all these adventures me and Arnie get into. I end up calling him "Dad." He asks me to.

I've got the first Terminator—*Terminator 1*—but it's not as good as *2*, not even close.

But I watched it. After it was over and the Terminator lowers himself into this boiling green slime and the last thing you see is just his thumb, meaning thumbs-up, I turned off the VCR, turned off the light, got into bed, closed my eyes—and right away went back to thinking about Goober in there.

Then after a while I thought I got up and went to her room.

The door was open. They were jumping up and down on the bed, naked. They kept telling me to come on up, it's fun.

But I didn't want to. But then I was up there anyway. We were bouncing really high, our heads bumping the ceiling. It was kind of fun. But then Hank wanted us all to hold hands like a happy family, so I jumped off and floated back to my bed and woke up and turned over and went to sleep again.

My friend Shawn called me this morning and said come over because he got Mortal Kombat 2 for his birthday yesterday. So I came over and we played and he kept beating me. So I quit. He laughed.

I asked him did he see on the news last night? Chuck Norris coming right out and admitting he's a homo? Admitting he likes to wear a bra?

Chuck Norris is like Shawn's big hero. He's got a poster on his wall from *The Hit Man*.

He said, "How about that Arnold Schwarzenegger, admitting he still wets the bed."

So we started arguing, like we always do, about who's better, Chuck or Arnie.

Shawn said he wished they would make a movie starring both of them against each other so we could find out the truth.

I said it wouldn't be a very *long* movie—

He jumped in, "Right, about two minutes. That's how long it would take Chuck to kick his ugly butt," and he starts moving all over the room doing karate chops and spins and kick punches, going, "Hah! Yah! Hah! Yah!"

I tried to explain to him. I said all that martial arts stuff would be like a joke to Arnie. He'd be standing there shaking his head. Then he'd just lift him straight up by his hair. Chuckie boy would be kicking and chopping away and Arnie would have this look on his face, shaking his head with this look of, like, *sadness*. He'd feel *sorry* for little Chuckie.

We talked about whether they'd use weapons and what weapons they'd use. I figured Arnie would go with an A-K 47, like he had in *Predator*.

Shawn said he'd need more than that.

"So what's Chuckles got?"

He goes, "Weell," with this secret little look on his face, "I was gonna wait and show you later. I was gonna surprise you." Then he went to his dresser and got something out of the top drawer and turned around with his hands behind his back. "All *Chuck* would need," he said, "would . . . be . . . *this*," and he brought his hands around and went into a crouch and aimed this actual, totally real pistol straight at my face, yelling, "Freeze, dickwad!"

I did.

I was sitting on the edge of his bed and I held up my arms and tried to speak but I couldn't. Nothing came out.

He kept crouching there, holding the gun in both hands, aiming it right at my forehead, with this little grin.

I finally got a word out. "Don't."

He yelled, "Hasta la vista, Schwarz-nigger!" and pulled the trigger.

I peed a little.

"Damn," he said. "Forgot to load it. Oh, well. Next time."

I wasn't even all that mad at him. I was too interested. "Lemme see it."

He tossed it over. I dropped it. It weighed a ton.

"Where'd you get it?"

"My uncle, for my birthday. He was in 'Nam."

"Kill anybody?"

"Shitloads."

"With this?"

"Some of 'em. Mostly with an M-16."

"What's this called?"

He stuck his hands on his hips. "That right there, my friend, is an Army standard-issue forty-five caliber automatic side arm."

"Say that again."

"An Army standard issue forty-five caliber automatic side arm."

"Does it work? If it had bullets?"

"Nah. He took out the firing pin."

I looked at it, turning it over. I was getting an idea for something.

I asked if I could borrow it.

"No way."

I told him he could borrow anything of mine he wanted.

"Nope." He came up and took it back.

"You can borrow my bike," I told him. He's got this cheap thing he rides around on and mine's a Kestrel.

"Sorry," he said.

I told him, "Okay, you can *have* my bike. I'll trade it for yours."

"Trade for good?"

"For a while."

"For good."

"All right."

"Trade bikes for good and you can borrow the gun for a day."

"For a week."

"One day. Take it or leave it."

I took it.

He tossed me the gun back but I told him no, I didn't want it for today.

I had some more thinking to do first.

Hank

In my chair, in my book, I came to *Ashkhabad*, capital of Turkmenistan, population 400,000, and rested my eyes for a minute before looking up Turkmenistan, and fell asleep and dreamed I was down at the park with Brian, trying to teach him how to hit, having him pitch to me from the mound, but the mound was a good six feet high and he was up there firing everything *by* me, laughing his little ass off . . .

Jean woke me, shaking my arm. She apologized and explained there were people in the other room and I was shouting rather loudly.

This was the second time she's had to wake me for shouting. I sat up and asked her if I said anything.

"Most of it I couldn't make out," she said, "but I did hear, very clearly, 'son of a bitch' and 'you little shit.'"

"Man, I'm really sorry," I told her. "I was having a bad dream."

"Clearly."

"About that kid."

"Brian?"

"Right."

She asked me to tell it.

So I did. She sat on the footstool with her head cocked, listening very seriously. I didn't think the dream deserved how seriously she was listening, but when I finished she told me it sounded "very revealing."

"You mean the meaning of it and all that?"

She nodded, slowly.

"So . . . what's it mean?" I asked, feeling a little nervous, the way she seemed to know.

"Well," she said, "I can tell you what Freud might say about it."

"Freud . . ." I'd heard of him. "How do you spell that?"

"F-r-e-u-d."

I looked it up. "You mean . . . let's see . . . '*Freud, Sigmund*, 1865 to 1939, Austrian physician who pioneered the study of the unconscious mind'? That Freud?"

"The very same."

"Okay. Go ahead."

Here's what she told me. She said the pitcher's mound—get this—was really Karen's breast. I almost laughed. Karen's got big hooters but come on. And she said Brian was standing on the mound because he was claiming possession of his mother and defending her from my sexual assaults.

I said, "*Assaults*?"

"From his point of view," she said.

"Yeah but . . . this was my dream," I reminded her.

"Which shows that at some level you understand—even empathize with—his point of view."

"I understand he's a little momma's boy. I understand *that*," I said.

"All boys, Hank, are momma's boys."

I poked my chest. "I wasn't."

"Well . . ."

"I was out playing *ball* everyday. This kid doesn't even leave the damn *house*. And in real life he couldn't strike me out if the mound was *fifty* feet high."

She nodded, listening.

"But go ahead," I told her. "What else?"

"Well, there's the bat, of course."

"Yeah?"

"An obvious phallic symbol."

"A what?"

"The bat in the dream is your penis, Hank."

"My . . ."

"And, of course, by striking you out, Brian is thereby rendering your member . . . well, useless."

"Now *wait* a second."

But just then somebody rang the little bell on her counter.

"Excuse me, Hank," she said, and hurried off to answer it.

I got out of the chair and went walking around the room, a little worked up. I felt like telling her to go ask *Karen* about my useless member, see what *she* tells you.

But when Jean came back all I said was I had to be going.

"You're upset," she said. "I'm sorry."

I told her I wasn't upset at all. "There's nothing to be upset a*bout*," I said, and gave a laugh, because there wasn't, so how could I be upset?

She stood there nodding her head in agreement.

"But I just wanna tell you something, Jean, okay? Before I go?"

"Certainly."

"Okay, in nineteen eighty-one I struck out a total of only eleven times the entire season, which set a new Midwestern A Division record, which, as far as I know, is still standing. Feel free to look it up. All right? That's all I want to say."

She kept nodding her head, like the best thing to do with someone like this is just be very agreeable.

That was with a Tigers farm club, that fewest strikeouts record. Thing is, though, my batting average that year still wasn't much, about 265 I think it was.

See, I was batting in the leadoff spot that year, taking a lot of pitches, drawing a lot of walks, like a leadoff batter should, so I was up there with two strikes on me a lot, and what I would do with two strikes on me, I'd choke up on the bat even more than I already was and just try to meet the ball, just make contact. But you have to swing the bat a *little* hard, so all I'd usually end up doing was grounding out somewhere. I might as well have struck out. In fact, I probably would've had a much better batting average if I just took my regular swing with two strikes and to hell with whether I whiffed.

Except, I just couldn't bear striking out. I had this real *dread* of it. Still do. For one thing, Nellie Fox hardly ever whiffed. He ranks as the fourth toughest batter to strike out in Major League history. The man averaged one K per 43 trips to the plate, an amazing mark. Plus, even if Nellie wasn't my model, there's just something about walking back to the dugout with my unused bat—my useless member—while the scorekeeper writes a big ugly *K* in the book by my name. I don't know if I'm feeling exactly *impotent*, as Jean would probably put it, but I'm definitely feeling like a totally worthless human being—a totally worthless piece of *shit*, in fact.

We won Saturday, 7–4, Brannigan going eight innings, Fitzgerald closing. Gordie put me in for the first two innings, then sat me for goddam Dunbar the rest of the game.

Which hurts. A lot.

Meanwhile, the Hounds From Hell had somehow lost their game over in Morton against the fourth-place Survivors, which meant we were now tied with the Hounds for first place, one game left to go, Wednesday night, and that game was against—you guessed it—the Hounds.

Gordie told us all this in the dugout before we left. He also told us we were a team of destiny. Those were his words. And he kept calling us "men." Like for example: "I believe that you men . . . are a team . . . of destiny."

Then Walter said he wouldn't be able to make it Wednesday, that he had to work late all next week.

Sometimes you have to feel kind of sorry for Gordie.

Then Dunbar said *he* wouldn't be there, either.

And I thought, All *right*.

Sunday was a real nice day, sunny but not so hot and humid like it's been. So we went on a picnic, just me and Karen, Brian at his dad's.

We didn't go very far, only to the picnic table under the tree in her backyard, but we did it right. She made chicken salad sandwiches and potato salad and deviled eggs, and then we set everything into this old-fashioned picnic basket she has and walked off into the yard like it was a big open field somewhere.

"Oh, look," she goes, "*there's* a nice spot," pointing towards the picnic table.

"Perfect," I said.

She even had a big checkered table cloth.

After setting everything out, we sat and I opened a beer and quoted Tony: "*Salut.*"

She sighed.

I put the can down. "What's the matter, babe?"

She looked off, the way she does. "What's missing from this picture?"

I tried to think. Pie or something? But she wouldn't be sad about that. Then I thought of it.

I pointed out to her that if Brian *was* here we wouldn't be *having* a picnic.

That didn't cheer her up much.

So I made a suggestion. It was something I'd been thinking about suggesting anyway. I said, "Listen, tomorrow's your weight group, right? Seven o'clock?"

"Seven-thirty."

"All right. Don't bother getting a sitter. I'll stay with him."

"No, Hank. That's a nice idea. But not yet."

I laid it on the table. I said, "Karen, look. Every time I ask you when we're getting married, what do you do?"

She shrugged.

"There. That's what you do. You shrug. Or change the subject. Or make a joke. But you don't answer."

"Point, please?"

"The point is, you don't think Brian's ready for me yet. That's it, isn't it?"

"Partly." She was carefully breaking little pieces off a potato chip.

I figured what the other part must be. "And *I'm* not ready yet for Brian, right?"

She nodded.

"Okay," I said. "I agree. I do. And that's why I think it's time we did something about it."

She looked up from her potato chip. "But if you force yourself on him, he'll just—"

"Nobody's doing any forcing, Karen. I'll just be baby-sitting, that's all."

"Child-sitting."

"He'll probably just lock himself in his room and not come out till you're home again—but at least for a while we'll be in the same house together, just the two of us. And that's a start, right?"

She sighed. "I don't know . . ."

I reached my hand across the table. "Because we *are* getting married. I'm right about *that*, ain't I?"

She took my hand and gave me a smile. And I don't know if I've mentioned this before, but Karen has about the nicest, prettiest smile you ever saw. She really does.

Anyway, she agreed to let me watch Brian. She wasn't real happy about it—but hell, come to that, neither was I.

I had to promise her, though, not to do anything foolish, like try to get him to play catch with me. Which I tried when I first met him and ended up saying something to him like, "What kind of a boy doesn't wanna play catch?" And he said something back like, "What kind of a grownup still plays *base*ball?" And that's about where we still stood.

Karen opened her can of Diet Coke and we drank a toast to our future—hers and mine and Brian's. "Happiness of all types and kinds," I said, quoting Tony again. And then we had ourselves a nice little picnic. Had some laughs. And I'll tell you something, this woman makes a wicked chicken salad sandwich. She even cut the crust off, like they do over in England. I *think* it's England where they do that. I'll have to ask Jean.

Brian

"No way, Jose! No day, I say! *Okay*?"

That's what I told my mom. But she said first of all her name wasn't Jose, and that I didn't have any say. Hank was going to be my sitter tonight. "End of discussion."

I couldn't believe it. I said, "Thanks a lot, Mom! It's real nice to be loved!" Then I went to my room and slammed the door as hard as I could, and opened it and slammed it again.

I called my dad and got his machine. I waited for the beep and yelled, "Dad! It's me! Brian! Help! Help!" and hung up.

Then I was gonna trash my room to show her how I felt, to show her what she was *doing* to me. But then I remembered my Plan.

This was perfect for it. We'd be alone. I'd have plenty of time. She wouldn't be back for a couple of hours. This was my chance. If I had the balls. Shawn said I didn't.

But like my T-shirt says, *Just do it.*

I went to the door and listened. She was in the kitchen fixing dinner. I snuck into the living room and got the camcorder down from the closet and snuck back and put it in my dresser and covered it up with socks. Then I went out to the kitchen.

She was at the counter by the sink, opening a can of tuna. I said, "Mom, I'm sorry I got mad and yelled like that, okay?"

She turned around. "Oh, honey, come here," she goes, and put out her arms.

I stepped in and she hugged me. I like how her boobs feel.

"I know this is all real hard for you," she said, kind of crying and stroking the back of my head. "I know," she said, "I know . . ."

When she was finished I told her I had to go over to Shawn's but I'd be right back.

"Well, I'm fixing dinner, hon."

"I'll be right back. I promise. Okay?"

"First give me another hug."

Riding over to Shawn's I felt kind of sad, this being my last ride on my bike. It's an 8-speed Kestrel CS-X with full suspension, carbon forks and airfoil tubing. Shawn's is this J.C. Penny piece of shit.

All set.

Camcorder on dresser, covered with pajamas except for the eye. Eye aiming at chair in front of TV.

Tape rolling.

TV on, sound turned off, picture scrambled.

Gun in right-hand bathrobe pocket.

Goober in front room watching baseball.

Just do it

Hank

Brian asked me to fix his TV picture. Asked me *politely*. Said "please." And I thought, Well hey, maybe this is how he says he don't hate old Hank too bad. Or maybe he just wants his TV fixed.

Anyway, I told him, "Let's have a look," and sat in his swivel chair in front of the set to see what I could do. The picture was bent out of shape and there wasn't any sound.

"Turn around," he said. "Look."

I looked over my shoulder.

He was standing by the door holding on to a pistol with both hands, aiming it at my face.

"*All* the way around!" he shouted.

I swung the chair around. "What's this, a stick-up?" Trying to treat it lightly. But I'll tell you what, the gun looked pretty damn authentic. "Should I get my wallet out?"

"Freeze!"

I did.

"Hands up!"

I put them up.

He seemed to be thinking what to do next, breathing quick, the pistol quivering a little.

"That a real piece ya got there, buddy?" I asked, in a casual manner.

"It's my dad's."

"Loaded?"

"Totally."

I believed him. I figured I'd better.

I said, "Brian, listen, okay? Now, I know you don't like me a whole hell of a lot. In fact, I know you kind of hate me. But, see—"

"Y'scared?"

"Little bit. Sure."

Fact is, my heart was pumping out that clammy kind of sweat I get and my held-up hands were shaking worse than his were.

"Know what my dad calls you?" he said.

"No, I don't."

"He calls you Goober. Know why?"

"No idea. But why don't you . . . why don't you put the gun down, Brian. Or just lower it, okay? And then you can tell me. Because, see, I can't *listen* very good when you're aiming—"

"Shut up!"

I shut up.

"I'm gonna shoot you now," he said, just like that.

I said, "Well, Brian, wait, what about—you were gonna tell me why your dad calls me—what was it, Gipper?"

"Goober."

"Right. Why's he call me that, Brian? That seems like a funny kind of a—"

"Hasta la vista, Goober!"

"Brian, don't. Please. Don't. I'm asking you. As a favor. Think about your mom. How mad she'll be. Please, Brian—"

"Beg," he said.

"I think I am, buddy. I think I'm begging pretty good here."

"Beg on your knees," he said.

"On my knees. Well. Okay. Sure. I can do that."

But it turned out I couldn't. I tried. I scooted to the edge of the chair, still keeping my hands up. But then I couldn't go the rest. There was just no way. I mean, I didn't do it for Jesus Christ that day in the bathroom and I sure as hell wasn't gonna do it for this fucking kid.

I let my hands down and sat there looking at him, hoping to God he wouldn't shoot me.

"On your knees!" he shouted, all redfaced and crazy-looking.

I shook my head: No.

He screamed, "I'll shoot! I'll shoot!"

I couldn't move or speak. I just sat there staring at him and he just stood there staring at me, both of us breathing hard . . .

Then his phone rang and I wet my pants. Little bit, anyway.

Brian

Goober tried to get me to answer it. He said maybe it's my mom having car trouble. "She needs a new starter," he said. "I keep telling her to bring it in and I'll—"

"Shut up," I told him.

I liked saying that and the way he obeyed.

The phone stopped ringing and you could hear the answering machine in the front room, but no message. I went back to work on him.

I wanted him down on his knees with his hands together like he's begging. I wanted him crying and begging on the floor, going, "Please, please, please." I wanted about two or three minutes of that. Then I'd show him the camcorder and tell him he better not come around here again or even call her on the phone because if he did I would send the tape to *America's Funniest Home Videos* so everybody in the whole country could see.

And I would, too. I'd erase everything except him begging on his knees, this totally grownup guy on the floor all whimpery like a little puppy dog, going, "Please, please, please." I know they'd use it. They have stuff on there not half as funny.

I closed one eye and aimed right at the middle of his forehead and told him he had five seconds to get down on his knees.

"Four . . . three . . . two . . ."

He stood up.

I yelled, "*One!*"

He started walking towards me.

I backed up against the door. I shouted, "Hasta la vista, baby!"

He kept coming.

"Hasta la vista! Hasta la vista!"

He stood there holding out his hand for the gun, looking me dead in the eye.

I put the gun in his hand and started explaining.

"It's not even loaded—it belongs to Shawn—his uncle gave it to him—he was in Vietnam—for our *country*—he took out the firing pin—it doesn't even shoot."

Goober looked at it.

"See?" I said. "A *joke*."

He looked at me.

I said, "What. Did you think I was serious? God, I'm sure!"

He was gonna hit me. I could tell from his face and the way he was breathing he was gonna hit me really hard.

I wanted my mom.

But all he did was give this big loud horrible yell like an animal and threw the gun across the room.

I quick opened the door in case he felt like leaving now. And he did. He left. He walked to the living room and out the front door and slammed it.

I waited a minute. Then I went to the living room and peeked through the curtains. His car was still parked out front. The porch light was on and I could see his legs. He was sitting on the steps. He was waiting for her. He was gonna tell.

I went out there.

You should have seen the back of his shirt, how wet it was.

I said to him, "Sorry. Okay?"

He didn't answer or turn or anything.

"Don't tell my mom," I said. "Okay?"

He still didn't say anything.

I even called him Hank. "Okay, Hank?"

He finally said something. "Beg," he said.

So I did. I said, "Please don't tell my mom?"

"On your knees," he said.

I got down on my knees and put my hands like praying. "Please don't tell my mom?"

He turned around and looked at me. "Get up," he said in this like real disgusted voice. Then he turned away again.

I got up and told him if he didn't tell my mom I would *do* something for him. A giant favor. I tried to think what.

It was right out there in front of us.

"I'll wash your car," I said. "And wax it. Make that baby shine." And that *would* be a giant favor because I didn't even know how, and plus you should see his car. Even in the day-time you still can't even hardly tell the color.

"Okay?" I said. "Deal?" I said. "Hank?"

"Wait here," he told me.

"All right," I said, being obedient.

He went over to his car and opened the trunk. I thought he was gonna get some rags and wax and stuff. But he took out a baseball mitt and a ball.

"Get in the backyard," he told me. "Let's go."

Hank

Honest to God, I actually had to tell him which hand to put the glove on—and he still looked like he had it on the wrong one.

I turned on the deck and the patio lights, then stood across the yard from him and held up the ball.

"Not hard!" he yelled, standing there in his bathrobe.

I'll tell you something, I was tempted. I really was. I felt like skulling him. I'm serious. For what he did to me tonight, I felt like shattering his fucking skull.

I lobbed it underhand.

He got out of the way, skipping to his right, holding the glove to his left, eyelids all a-flutter, the ball arcing over his glove and rolling to the fence.

"Pitiful. Go get it," I told him.

He went and picked it up, wanting to know how many more.

"Until you learn."

"What, my lesson?"

"How to catch, how to throw. Let's see your arm."

He held up his arm.

"I mean, *throw* the ball."

He swung back his arm, stepped with his right foot instead

of his left, swung his arm forward, released too soon and the ball sailed off towards the deck.

"Horrible. Go get it. *Move*."

He trudged over to the porch, picked up the ball and trudged back.

I told him, "Stand like this—*side*ways towards the target. Step forward, arm cocked. Foot comes down pointing straight so the hips can open, like so. Release the ball up here and follow through, end up facing front. Go ahead."

He threw it exactly like the other one and it sailed off towards the porch again.

"Get it. Go on. Try again. Only, *this* time—"

"Can't I just wash your car?"

"No. Let's go. Get the ball."

"*You* get it. I got the last one."

I looked at my watch, then over towards the driveway, like I was expecting his mom pretty soon.

He got the hint and went after the ball, bitching and moaning all the way there and back: "I *said* I'm sorry. God. It wasn't even loaded. Can't you even take a joke? Let me wash your car. This is stupid. I can't do this. I don't know how."

I asked him what about that egg he threw at the back of my head not so long ago. I said it seemed like that egg was thrown with some real authority.

He said he didn't remember any egg.

I said, "Sure you do. I was sitting on the couch with your mom. Remember? As a matter of fact, I was asking her to marry me. Or was just about to. I was about to say to her, 'Karen—'"

He flung the ball at my head, a bullet.

I was barehanded, so it stung like hell. "*Damn*," I said, shaking out my hand.

And you know what he did? I couldn't believe my eyes. He punched the pocket of his glove.

So right away I told him, "All right, here's a grounder now," and rolled him one a little to his left.

He sidestepped over, stuck the glove down, and the ball rolled in and rolled out.

"Two hands," I told him. "One hand catches, the other covers up."

His throw was right on line again—the mechanics still girly as hell, but we could work on that some other time. I didn't want to break the spell.

I told him, "Here's another grounder, but this time *two* hands, understand?"

He shrugged, like he still didn't give a shit, but he went right after the ball, got the glove down, and when the ball rolled in he covered up to keep it there.

"There ya go," I told him, wishing Karen would get back so she could see this.

His throw was high and off to my left and I had to jump for it, making a pretty fair grab.

"There ya go," he said.

It was taking some effort to stay mad at him.

I threw him a roller to his other side and he scooted over and took it in with both hands, and his return throw was on the mark.

I said, "That glove you're using, that's a Nellie Fox model. Ever hear of him?"

"No. Throw it in the air."

I lobbed it underhand and this time he stood his ground, flinching and blinking but hanging in there, and the ball hit the heel of the glove and fell to the grass.

"What'd I tell ya? *Two* hands. Always. Always."

He picked up the ball, looking pissed off, and flung it back, low, the ball skipping under my hand and smacking my shin.

"*Christ*," I said, and went hopping around.

"Two hands," he said.

I looked at him.

"Just *kid*ding. God!"

I rubbed up my shin. A baseball hurts like hell.

"C'mon," he said, putting up his glove again.

I told him, "Could you wait a second please? I'm in a little bit of pain here."

He gave a big sigh and dropped his arm.

"All right, all right," I said, hobbling back to the ball. "Ready?"

He nodded, glove up.

This time I tossed it with a little more loft.

And he caught it right in the pocket and covered up with his other hand.

I gave up trying to stay mad. "*Atta*boy, *there* ya go, *that's* it!"

And I'm not a hundred percent sure but I think he almost smiled.

Then he started to throw, but stopped. “Dad,” he said, and dropped the ball, shook off the glove and walked towards the deck.

Jim was there, in a suit and tie.

Brian

I went right over and told him, "He made me, Dad. He said I had to. But it wasn't any fun. I hated it. I hate baseball. Honest."

He said to me, real slow, "What in God's name was the idea, leaving me that message?"

I didn't know what he was talking about.

He goes, "On my voice mail? 'Help, help'?"

"Oh yeah," I said.

"Oh yeah," he goes.

He said he called but nobody answered—remember when the phone rang?—so he got in the car and drove all the way out. "And here you are," he said, "happily playing catch."

"I *wasn't* happy, Dad. I told you, I hated it. I was *un*happy. Honest. *Un*happy."

He said, "You're missing the point, Brian. Playing catch is not the point. I'll ask you again. Why did you leave me that message? As a joke?"

"No," I told him. "No joke."

"Then why. I want to know."

He probably wouldn't think Goober kid-sitting me was a good enough reason, so I was trying to come up with something, but it was hard with him standing over me like that.

I said, "Be*cause*."

He said "because" wasn't an answer.

Then I thought of one. I liked it. I said, "Because I was scared," and started breathing hard, like I was scared just remembering.

"Scared of what," he goes, and folds his arms, all set not to believe me.

"Of *him*," I said, pointing.

Goober was in the middle of stuffing a bunch of shaggy chewing tobacco in his mouth, from a little bag in his hand, and he stopped.

I said, "He had a gun, Dad! He came in the room and told me if I didn't play catch with him he'd blow my brains out! The guy's crazy! Take him to court! Sue him, Dad, sue him!"

He looked over at Goober, like saying, "Well?"

Goober spit some brown juice on the ground, like there's his answer.

And my dad looks back at me like I'm lying!

I said, "What, you believe *him* instead of *me*?"

"Brian, come on. He pulled a gun on you?"

"You believe *Goober* instead of your own son? Your own flesh and—"

"Now, don't start getting all—"

"Thanks a lot, Dad! It's real nice to be loved!"

I ran in the house and into my room and slammed the door. I thought about taking the gun out there to show him, but he probably *still* wouldn't believe me, and I dove on the bed.

My own father . . . my own father . . .

It wasn't just that he didn't believe me. That was bad, but you know what was worse? The thing that was worse? He wasn't mad at all about me playing catch with Goober. He didn't even seem like he *minded*.

Hank

Jim says to me, "You didn't, right?"

"Didn't what."

"Pull a gun."

I just looked at him.

"Didn't think so." He glanced at his watch. "Well, love to stay and have *more* fun—"

"Why don't you go in and talk to him?" I said. I felt like he should. Like *some*body should, what the hell.

"*He's* all right, take my word," he said. Then he goes, "Do me a favor, though. Don't tell me how to handle my own kid."

I didn't say anything to that.

"Understood?" he goes.

Tough guy.

I asked him, "Who's Goober?"

"Who's what?"

"Goober. That's what Brian calls me. He says *you* gave me the name."

"Brian says a lot of things, as you may have noticed." Then he looked at his watch again. "All right, I'm outa here," he said, and started walking away backwards, pointing at me. "Good seeing you. Always a treat. You play billiards?"

"No."

"Shame. Listen, hi to Karen for me. Gotta run." And he did, back to the street and his fucking Fiat.

After he'd gone I stood there for a while, thinking. Then I went in the house and knocked on Brian's door.

"It's Hank," I said.

"Beat it, Goober!"

I spoke through the door: "I just wanna say I enjoyed playing catch with you tonight and I think *you* enjoyed it too, so maybe we should do it again some time."

"Fuck you."

"When you're more in the mood."

I was out in the yard again, tossing pop-ups to myself, when Karen finally pulled into the driveway. I got rid of my chaw and went over and gave her a hug and a kiss.

"So how'd it go?" she asked.

"We played catch."

"No . . ."

"Yes, ma'am. And I'll tell you something. The kid ain't bad. Not too bad at all."

Brian

I rode over to Shawn's this morning on his J.C. Penny two-wheel dog turd and gave him his gun back. I brought the Goober tape over too. I was afraid to play it in my room, even while she was at work. Plus, I wanted Shawn to see it. I didn't get Goober on his knees, okay, but I tried, I didn't wimp out, and Shawn said I would.

He made a bowl of Jiffy Pop and we sat on the floor.

"*Terminator Three*," he goes, in this voice. "He's back. And this time—"

"C'mon," I told him. He had the remote.

He hit Play.

And there's my chair.

About a minute of that.

"Action-packed," Shawn goes.

Then you hear me off-camera, "Hank? Would you come here for a minute?" Then a few seconds later. "Would you fix my TV picture please?"

You hear Hank say, "Let's have a look."

And I say, "Thank you."

"What *is* this, *Mr. Roger's Neighborhood*?" Shawn goes.

I told him, "Shh. Watch."

Hank enters the picture and sits in the chair with his back to the camera.

You hear me tell him, "Turn around. Look."

He looks over his shoulder.

I told Shawn, "*Pause* it."

He did.

I said, "Okay, right now I'm standing over by the door holding the gun, aiming straight at his face. See how he looks kind of surprised?"

"Maybe you're standing there holding your wanger."

"Yeah? Watch."

He hit Play.

And right away a great scene. You hear me tell Hank to turn *all* the way around and he does, but then he tries to make it a joke and goes for his wallet, but I tell him "Freeze!" and he freezes, and I tell him "Hands up!" and he puts them up.

Shawn goes, "*Dag*."

Which is what he always says now when he's like really impressed with something. He got it from these black guys at school.

I was impressed too, you know? I mean, I couldn't believe I actually really did this, even to Goober.

Anyway so Goober's sitting there now with his hands up, going, "That a real piece ya got there, buddy?"

Buddy.

"It's my dad's," you hear me tell him.

"Good move," Shawn said.

Hank: "Loaded?"

Me: "Totally."

It's cool the way it's like just my voice, how he's sitting there talking to this guy you don't see.

The Voice wants to know if he's scared and he says, "Little bit," but he's scared a lot, you can tell.

I tell him my dad calls him Goober.

Me and Shawn both bust a gut.

Pretty excellent movie so far, you know? Action and suspense, plus a little comedy.

Goober tries to talk me into lowering the gun but I tell him to shut up, and he does.

Shawn looks at me and I know what he's thinking: *Dag*.

And now you hear me telling Hank I'm gonna shoot him. Just like that. "I'm gonna shoot you now."

He tries to stall.

The Voice yells, "Hasta la vista, Goober!"

Shawn spits up a gob of popcorn, laughing so hard.

Hank's going, "Please, Brian, don't," and so on.

The Voice tells him to beg.

He says he is.

The Voice tells him to beg on his knees.

And it looks like he's gonna obey. He scootches to the edge of the chair, with his hands still up, and it looks like he's gonna get down on the floor, but then he doesn't. He lets his hands down and just sits there.

The Voice yells, "On your knees, Goober!"

He shakes his head, no.

The Voice yells, "I'll shoot! I'll shoot!"

But he just keeps sitting there like a jerk.

Shawn goes, "Dag."

I tell him, "Pause!"

He does.

I ask him, "Why'd you say *that*?"

"Say what."

"'Dag,' like that. Who you talking about? *Goober*?"

"Well, I mean, ya gotta admit . . ."

"What. Admit what."

"The guy's showing some *balls* here, ya know?"

"I'm so sure! A total grownup against a kid with an empty gun. That takes a lotta balls. I'm so impressed. *Dag*."

"What's the difference if you're a kid, if you got a gun? And *he* don't know it ain't loaded. He thinks you're prob'ly gonna blow his brains out. Hang on, okay?"

He got up with the bowl—it was already down to mostly seeds—and went out to the kitchen. It's like totally impossible for Shawn to watch anything without popcorn.

So I'm sitting there by myself.

I didn't feel like looking at Goober up there on Pause. I just didn't feel like it, that's all. So I looked around the room at Shawn's stuff. He's got a lot, almost as much as me, but it's all shit brands, like his bike.

J.C. Penny.

Anyway, I sat there looking all the way around the room. Then I was back to the screen again. And I looked.

He's sitting up real straight on the edge of the chair, holding on to the arms real hard. His eyes are shut and his whole face all tight. Like I might really shoot. Like I might really blow his brains out. Like he might really die right there. But like he's not going down on his knees, no way . . .

Dag.

When Shawn came back I told him let's go do something.

"What about the movie?"

"The rest is boring. He just keeps sitting there. Let's go ride our bikes. Come on. You can ride mine, if you want."

He goes, "That's okay, I'll ride my own. I don't *like* J.C. Penny bikes."

I told him he was a dickwad.

Part Five

The South Suburban Times

SHARKS AND HOUNDS IN TITLE GAME TONITE

The Shopalot Sharks will take on the Haines Insurance Hounds From Hell tonight at 7:30 at Riverside's Heenan Field in a game that will decide the winner of the Southwest Suburban Adult Men's Baseball League.

In assessing his club's chances, Sharks manager Gordie Baumgartner sounded a dramatic note. "Let me just say that I believe we are a team of destiny," he stated.

Hounds skipper, Lou Pinazzo, seemed equally confident. "We're much better than them," he said.

League president Charles "Charlie" Landis expressed his delight with the close pennant race this year. "I'm delighted," he said.

Tommy

Jesus, the *people.* I was with Jerry—he traded shifts with Larry—and we couldn't even find a seat. We had to stand along the fence. I hate having to fucking stand. I was thinking about leaving, but then Chicklit came out of the dugout with a bat in his hands and I decided to stick around.

"Hey, has-been! Hey, never-was! Chicklit! Hey! I'm talkin' to you! Go back to bed, ya fuckin' loser!"

He got down on his knee in the on-deck circle.

"You *better* pray!"

Jerry joined in. "You're decrepit, Lingerman!"

I told him, "Take it easy, take it easy."

"What, you're the only one can fuck with him?"

I didn't answer that. I lit a cigarette.

Mitchell grounded out right away, and while Chicklit stepped up to the plate Jerry started giving him all kinds of shit, just to show me, calling him decrepit and a dink and a fag and a fucking weenie and everything else.

So I was glad when old Chicklit slapped out a single. I kept it to myself, though, naturally.

Mancini grounded into a double play to end the inning, and Christ you shoulda heard the Hounds heading back to their dugout, like a buncha animals.

"Complete, absolute, total fucking blowout," Jerry predicted, meaning the Hounds over the Sharks, and laid into Chicklit some more when he went out to his second base spot: "You're decrepit, Lingerman! Decrepit!"

Jerry gets a new word, he likes to break it in.

"Lingerman! Hear me? You're decrepit!"

I ended up violating one of my own personal rules of conduct: *Never make a bet in anger*. I told Jerry I was willing to wager the Hounds would choke to death on their own dog vomit.

He looked at me. "Twenty-five?"

"Fifty."

"Fifty it is."

He put out his hand to shake but I strolled away, leaving him like that.

A nice moment.

Stupid fucking bet, though. Jesus.

I went walking around. A very pleasant evening, nice little breeze. I bought coffee and a couple Slim Jims at the concession stand. Then I turned around and walked straight into this tiny old lady standing behind me, spilling about a gulp and a half on her head.

She went, "*Ah*," and covered up with her hand.

"Hey, didn't see ya down there. How ya doin'?" I said.

She took her hand down and looked at it.

"Coffee," I told her. "Extra cream, no sugar. You'll be all right. Enjoy the game."

I went over to the bleachers, see if any of these people in line left me their seat.

Jean

It seemed a kind of baptism: afterwards I felt much more a part of it all. The couple behind me asked if I was all right, and the woman at the counter lent me a clean rag to dab my hair. Someone suggested I sue the man. Someone else suggested I sue the concession stand. I bought a cup of hot tea and one of those enormous German pretzels.

I hadn't been to a baseball game since—well, since before my husband died, and that was thirteen years ago. I'm really not much of a fan, I'm afraid. So when Hank asked if I was coming to his championship game, I told him I had some letters to write.

In fact, that was true. And I was home at my desk writing to my friend Marge, who moved to Spokane some years back, when I realized how little there was to tell her since my last letter, a full month ago. So I wrote, "I went to a baseball game tonight," and put down the pen and drove to the ballpark.

My place in the bleachers was on the fifth tier from the bottom, at the very end, my blue windbreaker there as a marker. I went round to the front and, tea in one hand and that ridiculous pretzel in the other, began excusing my way up, rather wishing I had stayed put.

My friend John the Baptist was in the second row, near the end, gnawing on a dried meat stick. When he saw me coming, he covered his head. I smiled.

Then a collective groan went up—and a cheer from the other bleachers—in response to something taking place on the field, but I didn't dare look. And at last, all out of breath, I arrived. I thanked the man next to me for saving my place. He shrugged.

Out there under the lights Hank's team was just now returning to the field for the second time. The scoreboard beyond the outfield fence indicated there were still no points for either side—or *runs*, I should say.

I sipped my tea and nibbled at my pretzel.

This was so interesting, seeing Hank in this setting. I was first of all struck by how much older he was than the other players, most of whom looked to be in their twenties—and yet he seemed more energetic than any of them: raking the dirt with his cleated shoes, tugging at the bill of his cap, punching his mitt and even spitting into it—tobacco juice, I assumed from his distended cheek—and all the while shouting out encouraging little phrases to the pitcher.

So different from the quiet man at the library this afternoon, asking for my help in pronouncing *Azerbaijan*.

And I must say, I was also impressed with his skill out there. For example, when he took his turn as batter in the first inning he promptly made a safe hit, then later as a defensive player very nearly achieved a spectacular catch, giving chase to a ball and at the last moment throwing himself headlong, mitt extended, missing by inches—a valiant effort.

And yet, while he knelt there a moment catching his breath, a man along the fence continuously taunted him, calling him "decrepit."

You really have to wonder about people.

At any rate, as I said, there were no runs as yet for either side—but out there batting now was a huge, formidable-looking galoot with his shirt tail out, and after swinging mightily at a pitch and missing it altogether, he walloped the next one, sending the ball far and high and over the scoreboard. It was a home run, and the man began very slowly, very leisurely making his way round the bases, clearly "rubbing it in."

So, while everyone on the other side was cheering wildly, our side was roundly booing the fellow—not so much for his success as for his smug behavior. And with my heart beating high in my chest I set my tea and pretzel down, cupped my hands around my mouth, and cried out:

"Booo! Booo! Booo!"

But then someone among us went too far, tossing an empty liquor bottle onto the field.

Almost immediately a police car that was parked further along the fence gave a sort of burp on its siren, and we all fell silent. A uniformed officer emerged from the car and marched over.

In my mind I wrote to Marge: "At that moment I felt a curious mix of dread and delight."

Officer Phil

I stood in front of the bleachers, feet spread, hands on my hips—and wanted to say, "Folks, I have a confession to make," then tell them my secret. But I can't tell *any*one, not even Karen.

"Who threw the bottle?" I said.

This guy Tommy hollered, "Down in front!"

Got a big laugh.

Ordinarily I would have waited it out and asked again—a police officer is trained to maintain his composure—but instead I slapped my hand on the butt of my gun and yelled, "Who threw the goddam *bottle*? "

A dozen or so witnesses indicated the same suspect, sitting near the top, white elderly male, one Rudolpho Rossi, aka Rudy.

I told him, "Let's go."

He made his way down, weeping and insisting it was self-defense.

I got a loud round of boos from both bleachers as I led him away. I put him in the back seat and told him to go to sleep.

The Hounds almost scored again that inning, loading up the bases, but the Sharks managed to get out of it. Meanwhile Rudy did as he was told and was snoring away . . .

I rolled up the window.

I said, "Rudy?"

He went on snoring.

"*Rudy.*"

Dead drunk asleep.

So I told him my secret, beginning with how it happened:

From one of my sources at the Purple Angel I'd gotten the word she was back in town and where I could find her. I was after her for confiscating Hank Lingerman's television and a valued photograph. My cousin Karen had reported it. She wanted me to at least try and get the photo back—it's Hank as a kid with his hero Nellie Fox, former Sox player, long before my time.

They're getting married, by the way, Hank and Karen. Haven't set a date yet, far as I know.

Anyway, I found her at the address the guy gave me. She was alone in the apartment, wearing a soiled-looking terry cloth bathrobe. I told her she was under arrest for theft and began informing her of her rights. And she started telling me how gorgeous I am.

"You . . . are so . . . *gorgeous*," she says, walking up to me like she's in some kind of trance, slowly shaking her head in amazement . . . then slipping off her bathrobe.

I told myself, *You are an officer of the law! You are an officer of the law!*

She started touching my badge with her fingertips, and kissing it.

"Like it was part of my flesh," I told Rudy.

He went on snoring.

I told him she's been staying with me for three days now.

I told him she calls me Gorgeous.

I told him I call her Cupcake.

I told him I never used to like nose rings.

I told him about her milky little body.

I told him I didn't like how glad she acted when she heard it wasn't Lingerman who reported her.

I told him she says my cock is bigger than his, by far.

I told him again what she calls me: Gorgeous.

I told him how she acted when I was leaving for work today: wanting to know how long I'd be gone, exactly when I'd be back, like she'd be counting the minutes, missing me bad . . .

Somebody rapped on the window and I jumped about a foot.

Karen

Dammit, I *told* him not to go bothering Phil, and look at him there.

Well, that was quick. Phil must have told him to buzz off. He's got that drunk in the back seat. Also a pretty bad case of nerves, I'd say.

Now where's he heading? Oh, the concession stand.

I should just be glad he came tonight. I didn't even have to cut a deal. I said, "Brian, want to come to Hank's game?" And he shrugged and said, "I don't care," meaning yes. And even more amazing, he left his Game Boy at home.

He even talked to me a little.

"What's 'decrepit' mean?" he asked.

I said, "Well, sort of . . . old and worn out."

"Think Hank is decrepit?"

"No, I do not."

"Why's that guy keep calling him that?"

It was Jerry or Larry from the Palace.

"I have no idea, hon. Does it bother you?"

"No. I just wanted to know what it meant."

Later on he suddenly said, "Gross! You see that?"

We're perched, by the way, on the very top tier of the bleachers, by his request.

"See what?" I said.

"Hank. He spit in his mitt—to*bacco* juice."

"Yuck," I agreed.

"Why'd he do that?"

"Conditions the leather?" I offered.

"I'm sure."

"Or maybe so the ball will stick better. You should ask him."

"Guess what, I'm not using that mitt again. I'm not even touching it."

"Well, maybe what we need to do is get you a mitt of your own," I said. "What do you think?"

He shrugged. "*I* don't care."

This was pushing it but I said, "Maybe you and Hank should take a drive out to the mall one of these nights. See what they've got."

After a moment he said, "You'd come too, right?"

"Oh, I think I'd just be in the way," I said.

That gave him another pause. Then he wanted to know who'd be paying for it.

"Well, Hank and I. Both of us," I said.

"What about Dad?"

"I think Hank and I can handle it," I told him.

He was quiet again.

Then this huge, arrogant guy hit a home run, everyone booed, that drunk threw a bottle, and Phil came over.

Brian's never been very impressed with Phil, in spite of the gun and the badge. I think it's because Phil talks so much when he drops by. Chitchats, in fact. Terminators don't chit-chat. But here he was, swearing and almost pulling out his gun, then throwing the criminal in the car—Brian enjoyed all that, I could tell. So when he said he was going to the concession stand I told him don't go bothering Phil, and watched him walk straight over there.

But I'm going to pretend I missed it. I don't want to get into a scrap with him here. And when we get home I'm planning to give him the news.

As I'm saying goodnight, I'll tell him.

I'll say, "Honey, guess what . . ."

Or, "Brian, there's something you should know . . ."

Or, "Hey, almost forgot to tell ya . . ."

I'll see.

Anyway, the news is, Hank and I are getting married a week from Saturday.

We decided last night in bed. Or I did. Then I shook him awake.

"Whatsa matter!" he said.

I said, "Will you marry me, say, a week from Saturday?"

He didn't answer right away and I couldn't see his face in the dark, so there was this moment . . .

Then he put his arms around me.

We're going to a JP at the Town Hall and reserving some tables at Antonio's for that night, with a buffet. I called Tony about it this afternoon.

"And what about a nice big banner on the wall," he said. "'Congratulations to Stromboli and Karen.'"

I said, "That *would* be nice. But I think 'Congratulations to *Hank* and Karen' would probably be—"

"No," he said. 'Congratulations to Stromboli and Karen.'"

"But, see, you're the only one who calls him that, Tony."

"That's right," he said.

It seemed to matter to him a lot.

So I told him, "Okay. 'Stromboli and Karen.' We'll go with that."

"Whatever," he says.

Then I got off before he could ask about being Best Man, Hank having gone with George.

Hank asked him this morning at work. He said George looked flustered and told him he'd have to think about it—a rather odd response, I thought, but Hank said he's just very careful, especially concerning white people. He said George came over later on and told him he'd be glad to do it, and they stood around for a while discussing what's wrong with baseball players nowadays.

We're sending Hank's dad a pair of plane tickets: for him and the mysterious Carlotta.

I said to Hank last night, "Wouldn't it be funny if it turned out she really *is* beautiful and young and sexy?"

He didn't seem to think that would be very funny at all.

I said, "Why not? Because *I'm* so ugly and old and fat?"

He said, "Hey, you're not so damn old."

I put my pillow over his face and laid on top of it with all my considerable weight—joking around, of course. But not entirely, not entirely. Anyway, I got off before he stopped struggling.

And here's the lucky groom-to-be right now, walking up to bat again.

He got a nice little hit his first time up, and afterwards I couldn't help elbowing Brian, saying, "How ya like *that*, huh?"

"It didn't go very *far*," he said.

He'd be even less impressed this time. Hank bunted. And was out. Close, though. And right away there goes Gordie running over to the umpire, yelling, "Why are you doing this to me? *Why*?"

And there's Hank drawing him away by the arm, Gordie still shouting over his shoulder, "*Why?*"

Hank walked him all the way back to the dugout.

That was nice. I wish Brian was here to see that.

Where *is* he, by the way . . .

Ah, here he comes. Fresh from the concession stand. He's got himself a tricky little climb ahead, with one of those monster pretzels and a cherry snow cone.

He looked all the way up before he started and I gave him a big wave with both arms. He tried hard not to smile.

He's going to be all right. I know he is.

Mary

Dear Phil,

Sorry about taking your stuff. I guess I don't realy think your gorjous. Oh well.

Please return this picture to Hank. We couldn't sell it and he probibly wants it back.

If you come after me I'll tell your boss you fucked me insted of arresting me—ok?

Well bye.

Sincerely yours,

M.

P.S. Tell Hank I said hi!!!

Gordie

I put it to Brownie, "Why are they doing this to me?"

"Who's that, Coach?"

"These *umps*. They don't just suck. There's something going on here."

"How do ya mean?"

"Money from the Hounds, I mean."

"That's a real possibility."

"Or they *put* money on the Hounds."

"Another possibility."

"Or else they just plain fucking hate me."

"Wouldn't surprise me a bit."

I looked at him.

"Just agreeing, Coach."

I sent him after a bag of sunflower seeds, to get rid of him. He'll be a while, with this crowd. Must be three hundred people out there. Probably they all read the paper today: *Let me just say that I believe we are a team of destiny.*

Man, we gotta win. We just fucking *gotta*.

Lord, how about it? We're heading into the bottom of the seventh here, down two to nothing, their big guns coming up again. But You know that. You know all things. And can *do* all things. You're the greatest, Lord, and I'm not just saying that. So how about it? Just get us through this inning, that's all I'm asking. Tell You what. Get us through this inning and I'll quit jacking off for a week. For a week, Lord. Whaddaya say.

It looked like maybe we had a deal, Brannigan getting two strikes on the batter right off, but then the asshole singled to left, and then he stole second, and then he went to third on a wild pitch.

Thanks, Lord.

"Time out!"

I went out to the mound to settle Brannigan down. Settle myself down, too. Gotta stay in charge here, stay on top: you're the boss, you're the driver, the guy at the wheel . . .

"How ya feeling, Bran Man?"

"Fine, fine, fine"—like I'm out here bothering him.

I told him, "Listen, I wanna keep you in all the way. I don't want any part of Fitzgerald. The guy's a fucking chokemeister. So whaddaya say? Can ya do it for me, big guy?"

Gives me a little nod.

Would it kill him to say something like, "Sure thing, Coach." Or kill *any* of these guys? Brownie's the only one shows respect, but he makes me sick.

I told Brannigan, "Let's play it safe. Walk this guy. He already doubled off you once and we got first base open, so let's put him on."

Not even a nod.

"Ya hear?"

Nothing.

"Can ya fucking answer me please?"

"I hear you."

"Attaboy."

I gave him a friendly slap on the butt to keep up appearances and trotted back.

Redman, I hope you're laying in the rain somewhere with a fucking tomahawk stuck in your skull.

Back in the dugout I yelled to my catcher Burlson and gave him the intentional-walk sign and he did what he's supposed to: stood up and held out his right arm for Brannigan to lob the ball outside. But Brannigan shook his head, and Burlson squatted back down again.

I don't believe this. I do not believe this . . .

Sure enough, Brannigan goes ahead and pitches to the guy—and *see*? See what fucking happens?—base hit up the middle and the runner on third goes dancing home.

"Time!"

I went out there again.

No way I'm taking this shit.

"Fitz! Get in here! Now! Let's go!"

I stepped onto the mound and told Brannigan to go take Fitz's place in right field, holding out my hand for the ball. "Go on. You're through here."

But he didn't go, or give me the ball. Just stood there looking towards the plate.

Stay calm. You're the boss. You're the driver.

"Let's go," I told him, hand out, wiggling the fingers.

"No," he says.

"Whaddaya mean, no? Gimme the fucking *ball*, dude!"

But he wouldn't.

Meanwhile here comes Fitzgerald crossing the infield, Lingerman with him, Burlson walking up from the plate, the ump right behind, and three hundred people in the stands all watching this little comedy skit, center stage under the lights.

So now I'm like, "Brannie, I'm asking you, okay? Cuz, see, I'm lookin' kinda funny standing here like this, front of all these people. So will ya please just gimme the fucking *ball* please?"

Shakes his head, no.

"Lingerman, tell him to gimme the ball."

"Bran, give him the ball. Go ahead."

So you know what Brannigan does? He looks at me—and hands *Lingerman* the ball. Gives it to *him*. Front of all those people. And walks off towards right field.

"Here you go," Lingerman says, holding out the ball for me to give to Fitzgerald, since I'm supposed to be the manager, you see. The driver. The guy at the wheel.

But I've had enough. I have finally fucking had enough.

"*You* give him the ball. I quit," I tell Lingerman, and walk off the mound and off the field, through the gate, past the bleachers, people shouting shit.

Tommy's in there and yells, "Have a nice destiny!"

The Palace was empty, Larry behind the bar with his newspapers.

Three beers later I'm crying and I just wanna know one thing: Why's everyone against me?

The umps. The fans. My own players. God. Everyone. Always. Why? What'd I do?

"Larry, can you tell me something?"

Keeps reading.

"Will you talk to me please and tell me something?"

"Tell you what?"

"Why's everyone against me? Can ya answer that? Why me? Ya know? Why . . . the fuck . . . *me*?"

"Why the fuck not? Listen what happened to *this* guy," he says, and starts reading to me.

But I'm not listening.

Redman

Billy went outside to throw up and hasn't come back. Wonder if he's passed out. I should go see. Bring him a blanket. Right after this beer . . .

He's taking me tomorrow to see Laughing Dog, out in the hills. Billy says he's very old and blind and wise. He says he learned his medicine from Black Elk.

Think of it. From Black Elk.

I really appreciate everything Billy's done for me. All I did for *him* was stop and give him a lift, and in fact I had no choice: he was standing in the middle of the road—young longhaired guy in a backwards ball cap—waving his scrawny arms, yelling, "Stop, man!"

I figured it was some emergency, but he got in the car very casually and said, "Hey, wasichu. Where you headed?"

Truth is, I was thinking about heading home. I'd never seen this kind of misery. People dead drunk asleep along the road. Little kids in their underwear crying in the dirt in front of houses you could topple with a sneeze. I even saw some people living in a gutted car out in a field, I'm not kidding. And here I was, in my BMW, in my chinos and L.L. Bean boots, searching for a spiritual mentor. I felt like a damn fool.

Still, I got a little defensive when Billy right away called me "wasichu," which means "white man," and I explained that in spite of my appearance I'm only part (15/16th) wasichu, and the rest pure Sioux.

He said, "Well, hey, brother," and gave me his hand to shake.

I was moved.

He said his name was Billy Kills-in-Water.

I said mine was Bob . . . Throws Smoke.

He said it was a good name.

I said yes, we both had warrior names.

He said we should have a drink together.

I agreed.

He directed me to a road that led to a town just off the reservation, where I could buy beer. He said I might as well get a case, so I did and we drove back to his trailer, drinking on the way, and continued to drink and talk until almost morning.

I told him about my great desire to follow the path of the spirit, and that I was searching for someone who could show me that path and guide me along it.

That's when he told me about Laughing Dog. He said he would take me out to see him, maybe the next day. Anyway, soon.

That was a week ago. I've been staying here since, sleeping on the couch and eating Billy's meals. I buy the food and he prepares it.

Yesterday he made a huge pot of chili that we brought over to a trailer down the road where his friends John and Michael Walking Eagle live. And get this, the three of them drummed and sang for me. What an experience. All I can say is, I kept my mouth shut about ever having done any drumming and singing myself. I truly felt as if any moment Sitting Bull and Red Cloud and Crazy Horse were going to suddenly appear in the room, drawn from the sky by the power and intensity of the singing—by its sheer *wochangi*.

Along with the chili, Billy and I had brought two cases of beer, so after the songs the four of us sat around drinking and talking. And for a while the brothers were very nice to me. I told them about my quest and they seemed to respect me for it. I was surprised they didn't recognize Laughing Dog's name when I mentioned it, but then Billy spoke to them for a moment in Lakota and they said to me, "Right. Laughing Dog. Yes. Very wise."

Later on, though, as we continued to drink, they became rather sarcastic, especially about my name, Throws Smoke, which they seemed to find very amusing, even after I explained its meaning.

And that's been the pattern with most of the others I've met. They're very courteous at first and rather shy, but as they drink up the beer Billy insists we always bring, their attitude towards me becomes more and more sarcastic.

And when Billy joins in with their laughter, I feel very alone.

But all in all, as I said, I'm very grateful to Billy, and he promises we'll definitely go see Laughing Dog tomorrow. He said he just hoped Laughing Dog would be home, as he often goes on long journeys.

"An old blind man?" I said.

"*Spirit* journeys," Billy explained.

I felt foolish.

He said if it turns out Laughing Dog is gone, he knew where we could stay while we waited for him to return from The Land of the Elders.

That's how he put it: The Land of the Elders. And I thought: This is really it. This is no workshop at the Holiday Inn. This is the real deal.

Billy added that we should probably make a beer run in the morning and just fill up the whole trunk, in case we need to stay with people for a while.

I asked him about that, if it was necessary to bring so much beer everywhere we went.

He said it's traditional.

I asked him how I should address Laughing Dog tomorrow and if calling him "Grandfather" might seem a little too familiar, at least at first.

"Whatever," he said, popping open a fresh can.

"Does he have a wife?" I asked, just curious.

He said Laughing Dog has three wives: Ellen Cooks Good, Betty Cleans Good, and Alice Fucks Good.

I think sometimes Billy enjoys pulling my leg a little.

Then he said he had to go throw up and went outside and hasn't come back. I should see if he's okay. Bring him a blanket. After this next one . . .

I wonder how Janet's doing. I sent her a postcard yesterday. I didn't know what to say to her:

Hi, Jan—
Doing fine. Hope you are too. Staying
with a guy named Billy Kills-in-Water.
Guess I'd better not go swimming
with him—ha ha.
Bob

I just realized something. This is Wednesday night. The Sharks are out there playing right now.

I wonder who's on the mound. Probably Brannigan. Or if he got in trouble, Fitzgerald . . .

What the fuck am I doing here?

No.

Don't start that.

Don't start.

Don't.

Tomorrow you'll be with Laughing Dog, who learned his medicine from Black Elk. Think of it, from Black Elk!

And you know something? I didn't tell Billy this but I have a very strong feeling Laughing Dog's been expecting me. I'm serious. I have a feeling when we meet he'll say:

My son, I had a dream that you were coming.

Then he'll pat the ground and tell me:

Sit here. And listen to my words.

And I'll say to him quietly, with all my heart:

Yes, Grandfather.

Hank

I was holding the ball and everyone was telling me what to do, so I figured I must be the new manager.

Mancini wanted me to get Brannigan back on the mound.

But Gordie did the right thing yanking him.

Mitchell said *he* wouldn't mind pitching.

But who would play short?

Fitzgerald told me to put anyone in to pitch but himself.

The ump wanted *some*body in or he'd call delay-of-game.

I gave the ball to Fitz.

"Aw, Jesus," he goes.

His first pitch sailed off into the backstop and the runner trotted to second base, clapping and hooting.

Fitz turned to me with his arms spread, meaning, *See?*

I told him to hang in there.

The batter belted his next pitch over the left field fence.

"Hank, get me out of here."

I went over. Thing is, with a little self-confidence Fitz is actually a pretty adequate pitcher. I asked him about his motto. "How's it go again?"

He sighed and recited, "'Just do your best. That's all you can do.'"

"All right, then."

"But I get these *grem*lins."

"Oh?" I wasn't sure I wanted to hear this.

"Little voices, whispering at me."

"Well . . . we all get that."

"Really?"

"Hey, Redman used to hear dead Indians."

"So what do *your* voices say?"

I was wishing Gordie hadn't quit.

"They say, 'Just do your best. That's all you can do.'"

"Aw, see, *mine* go, 'You're gonna fuck up, you're gonna fuck up, you're gonna—'"

"*Gentlemen?*" the ump called out to us.

I told Fitz to ignore his gophers.

"Gremlins."

"Whatever. Just ignore 'em. And keep the ball low."

It took a while, and another run, but he managed to get three outs, and we headed in for the top of the eighth, down 5–0.

I waited until everyone was in the dugout, then asked for their attention. "Okay, as you probably know, Gordie decided to quit."

"Good fucking riddance," from Brannigan.

"So, for the time being anyway, I guess I'm—"

"Question," Wilson said, raising his hand like a kid in class.

Brownie said to him, "Can it wait? The man's trying to speak. Go ahead, Hank."

"All right. Well—"

"They gonna get trophies?" Wilson asked.

"Nah," Lavinski said. "Just a little patch saying they're this year's champs."

I said, "See, that's what I wanna talk to you guys about."

"Trophies?"

"No, the *game*. I'm not so sure this thing is over, you know?"

"Ain't over till it's over," Brownie threw in.

"That's right," I said.

Burlson wanted to know who that's a quote from.

Brownie said he made it up.

Everyone started yelling he was full of shit.

Lavinski said it was from Ernie Banks.

Mancini said Leo Durocher.

Fitz said Howard Cosell.

"It was Yogi Berra," I said. "Now *listen*, will ya? Jesus."

They all got quiet.

Which threw me a little, but I told them, "Don't be swinging at the first pitch up there. Wait'll he gets a strike on you. He's starting to tire. See if we can draw some walks. We need baserunners. Lots of 'em."

"That it?" Mancini asked, set to go bat.

"No." I wanted to finish with something a little inspiring. I reminded them that this was it, for the league championship, two innings to go—

And Brownie jumped in, "So there's no tomorrow!"

Which is what I was gonna say.

So now they started on about "There's no tomorrow," who's *that* a quote from.

I went out to coach third base.

Mancini drew a walk, like I said to try and do. Which made me feel good, you know? Like they really thought of me as the manager. And hell, why not? All the years I been playing this game? All the years . . .

Wilson looped a single to left, Mancini pulling up at second.

I yelled to our dugout, "*See*? We're still *in* this! Get up! C'mon!"

And they did, they got up and made some noise. And even after Brannigan struck out they stayed on their feet. But then Ross popped out to short and everyone sat back down, except of course for Brownie.

Two pitches later, though, they were up again because Lavinski jumped on a hanging curve and launched it deep into right center field, everyone shouting at the ball, "Get outa here! Get outa here!" And it did. It got out.

And listen to that crowd.

I looked to see Karen. She was up there yelling along with the rest, shaking Brian by the arm like *he* was cheering too.

In a week and a half she'll be my wife.

My wife, Karen.

Sounds good, don't it?

My wife, Karen.

My stepson, Brian . . .

I turned around in time to give Lavinski a whack on the ass as he jogged on by.

Burlson flied out to end the inning.

So: 5–3.

Ain't over till it's over.

Fitz got into some trouble, walking the first two batters, but then struggled like hell against his gremlins, and we returned for the top of the ninth with the score still 5–3.

Brownie quoted from Gordie: "This is it! This is it! Do or fucking die!"

Fitz led off, and whiffed.

Top of the order now, Mitchell up, me on deck.

And after taking a called strike Mitch sliced a high shallow fly, the second baseman and the right fielder both calling for it, then both letting the other one take it, the ball falling safely between them.

Brownie shouted, "There's our break! There's what we needed! Up to you now, Hank! Up to you, old buddy!"

Shit.

This kid on the mound was a junkballer and he started me off with some kind of flutterball that I let float by. Ump called it a strike. Looked high but never mind.

Dig in. Focus. Here we go . . .

Another flutterball and I slapped it foul.

Two strikes on me now. Gotta protect. Anything close, go after it. Watch for that floater again. Here we go . . .

Waist-high fastball straight down the middle of the plate and I stood there watching it.

"*Striiike!*"—like an ice pick in the heart.

I walked back to the dugout.

"Nice going, Chicklit! Way to come through!"

"You're decrepit, Lingerman! Decrepit!"

I put my bat in the rack, helmet on the shelf, went to the far end of the bench and sat there.

Brownie came over. "Not *your* fault, Hank. This ump is terrible. Pitch looked a mile outside."

I told him to go away, please.

He went away.

I sat there staring between my feet, feeling worthless, completely worthless . . . a worthless piece of dried-up dog shit . . . of dried-up, *decrepit* dog shit . . .

Ping of the bat, the ump shouting, "Foul, out of play!" Then, "I'm all out! Gotta *have* one! Here ya go, kid. Toss it over."

I looked and he's talking through the wire fence to Brian, who's holding a ball in one hand and an ice cream bar in the other.

"Go a*head*," the ump told him.

He tried. The fence is about ten feet high there and he reared back, stepped with the wrong foot, threw—and the ball hit the fence about two feet from the top.

"Get it," the ump said. "Come on. Chop, chop."

Brian took a step towards the ball and hesitated, then turned around and walked off. Some other kid ran up and threw the ball over.

Ump said, "Attaboy."

I watched Brian walking away. And you know what he did? He threw down his ice cream bar. Just threw it down and kept walking.

That got to me. It really did.

I got up off my worthless ass and went after him.

He was out behind the concession stand. There's this little group of trees back there and he was sitting under one, arms folded.

"Hey," I said, walking up.

He looked at me and looked away again.

I stood over him. "Listen, you're never gonna throw worth a damn if you don't learn to step with your *left* foot, like I told you."

He kept sitting there staring off.

"But hey," I said, "you almost got it over. So just work on your mechanics and you'll—"

"Got a dollar?" he said.

It took me a moment before I could answer, this being a first. Brian asking me for money. Asking *me*. Goober.

"No," I told him. "What for?"

"I dropped my ice cream bar."

I corrected him, "You threw it down."

"It slipped!"

"You were mad," I said. "You didn't get the ball over the fence and you were mad at yourself. Disgusted. I know the feeling. I just struck out back there. Didn't even swing, just stood there looking at it. If I got on base I could have been the tying run."

"I'll pay you back," he said. "*God.*"

Just then all kinds of shouting went up from the field, and the Hounds started chanting like a bunch of goddam football players: "*We're number one! We're number one! We're number one!*"

"Hear that?" I said. "That's the other team. We just lost. I struck out and now we lost. And I'll tell you something. Just between you and me? It hurts."

I sat down against the other side of the tree.

"*We're number one . . . !*"

"Hurts like hell," I said.

We sat there.

After a minute he said, "How come you're always spitting in your mitt?"

"Nellie Fox used to spit in his," I answered.

"Who's Nellie Fox?"

"Guy I once played catch with."

"So why'd he spit in his mitt?"

"I don't know."

"You don't?"

"No."

"You just do it because *he* did?"

"That's it."

"What's he, your big hero or something?"

"Could say."

We sat there . . . .

"Know who Arnold Schwarzenegger is?" he asked.

"Big guy? Talks funny?"

"Yeah? Guess what. He could *kill* Nellie Fox. All he would do, he would just, first he would just—"

"He's already dead, Brian."

"Yeah, well . . . if he wasn't."

We sat there . . . .

"So when did ya play catch with him?"

"Long ago."

"You shoulda asked him."

"What."

"Why he spit in his mitt."

"I should've asked him a lot of things."

"Too late now."

We sat there until Karen found us.

When I got back to the dugout for my glove, everyone was gone and there was all the equipment—which I forgot was part of my job now. Not even Brownie had stayed to help.

I sat on the bench, just for a minute—a little tired, I'll admit. Bone-weary, in fact. The Hounds had finished chanting and slamming each other around and were gone, the field looking very peaceful now, nobody out there . . . until next spring . . .

I'll be back. I'm not *that* tired. Not yet.

I pushed myself up and started gathering bats and balls and helmets and catcher's gear, stuffing it all into a couple of canvas duffel bags . . .

Nellie, how come you're always spitting in your mitt?

Don't really know, Hank. Just something I do.

Funny thing is, I'm older now than *he* was that day—a lot older, in fact. Hell, a few years more and I'll be as old as him when he died.

I sat down again, holding a shin guard . . .

I'll tell you something, though. I can still remember that day we played catch. A lot of it I'm not real sure about, I mean fact from fiction. Like I said, I've told it many times in many ways. But you know what I remember? Something I definitely do remember? How *happy* Nellie seemed. I remember that. Smiling, relaxed, his cap tilted back—like this was exactly what he wanted to be doing right now: playing catch with me. Like that was the reason he came to the ballpark today: to toss me pop-ups and grounders. And like there wasn't any hurry. Like we had all the time in the world.

You know?

All the damn time in the world.